THE HEAT OF THE MOMENT

Margaret Carr

CHIVERS

British Library Cataloguing in Publication Data available

This Large Print edition published by BBC Audiobooks Ltd, Bath, 2006.
Published by arrangement with the Author

U.K. Hardcover ISBN 978 1 405 64066 4
U.K. Softcover ISBN 978 1 405 64067 1

Copyright © Margaret Carr, 2005

Printed and bound in Great Britain by
Antony Rowe Ltd., Chippenham, Wiltshire

CHAPTER ONE

Frances gardiner had only applied for the job of secretary to the internationally-famous three-day event rider, Kane Harding, because Martin Truscott, her employer and friend, had pointed out the advertisement in a popular riding magazine.

'It would be just the thing, Fran,' Martin had encouraged. 'A change of scene to get you out of racing for a time.'

Now, three weeks later, Frances allowed the letter of acceptance to flutter to the desk top. She rubbed a weary hand across her eyes, not quite believing what she had read. Through the window in front of her she could see down the yard and the horses, heads bobbing and weaving above their stable doors in anticipation of the midday feed.

The letter offered her a good wage and accommodation in return for long hours and a time schedule frequently overlapping at the Harding Ranch in Tenerife.

Frances chewed at her lips. She hadn't really expected a reply, let alone an outright offer. Unconsciously, she rubbed both arms where they had been broken sixteen months before in a riding accident. The accident had put an end to her racing career for the time being.

1

The specialist had advised a change and this job in Tenerife would certainly be that. Martin had been very kind finding another place for her here at the stables but she knew she wasn't pulling her weight and racing establishments, especially one that had only been going a short number of years, could not afford to carry dead wood.

Martin popped his head around the door of the tack room.

'Are you planning to eat with us today?' he asked brightly.

'Coming.'

Frances retrieved the letter and stuffed it into a pocket.

There were four lads living in the farmhouse and another four in the bothy at the entrance to the yard. All ate their midday meal in the farmhouse kitchen, but it was still empty when Martin and Frances entered.

Martin moved around the kitchen, taking off the slightly-damp tweed jacket that smelled of moorland and horses. He was a short man, of stocky build and in his late thirties. He and his wife, Tessa, were more of a family to her than any blood relative she had ever had. Tessa was heavily pregnant with their first child and it struck Frances that if she took this job she would miss the baby's arrival.

Before she could change her mind she whipped out the letter.

'There's something I want you to see,' she said, holding the letter out towards Martin.

He left what he was doing and came across to the table.

'Good heavens,' he said after he had read it. 'What did you put in that application? You certainly impressed him. Never even took me up on a reference. Pity that, I had one all ready.' He grinned at her. 'Clever you.'

'You think I should go then?'

'Don't you? I mean, aren't you happy about it?'

The smile vanished to be replaced by a frown.

'Not many people can walk into a good job like that so easily.'

'I know, and that's what's bothering me. Don't you see? He didn't take up any references or arrange an interview or anything. Why?'

'Well, he does live in Tenerife when all is said and done, though with all this technology around I must say I am a bit surprised he couldn't find a better way to contact you. You did use the headed paper with fax and e-mail information, didn't you?'

'Of course.'

'Perhaps he's a devil to work for and you were his only applicant.' Frances raised her eyebrows in disbelief.

'Look, does it matter why he chose you? The letter is signed and dated. It even gives

3

you the name of a bank to draw your air fare from.'

'So you don't think there is anything odd about it?'

'No, I don't think so.'

'Right then, l"II go.'

'If you think there might be something fishy,' Martin added thoughtfully as he picked up the teapot, 'then buy yourself a return ticket.'

Frances gave him a beautiful smile, lighting up her pale face with its deeply shadowed dark blue eyes. In height, she was not far short of Martin, yet her bones had no more weight than a bird's and no matter how much she ate, she always stayed the same.

Her dark hair was tied up in a ponytail and swung in a fat ringlet as she walked. She had taken much teasing from the lads when she first started, but in time she had won their respect and affection and she would miss them.

Tessa walked into the kitchen carrying a heavy box of books. The kettle crashed on to the stove and Martin shot across the room to prise the box from his wife's arms.

'What have I told you!' he scolded.

Tessa sat down on a chair by the table and winked at Frances.

'Have you two been planning behind my back?' she asked, her head perched on one side like an inquisitive bird.

'Yes, we have,' Martin replied. 'Fran has been offered the Harding job.'

'You haven't. Oh, Fran, that's super, and such a gorgeous man, too.'

'How do you know he's gorgeous?' Martin asked, dipping over the back of the chair to plant a firm kiss on his wife's cheek.

'Because, oh, worldly wise, he came to stay at the Running Fox in the village many moons ago when I was a receptionist there.'

'What was he like, Tessa?' Frances asked.

'Tall, dark, long, straight hair that fell on to his collar. Latin-ish really except for those eyes. They were the kind of eyes you never forget, know what I mean—so bright they look unreal.'

'Like Paul Newman, you mean.'

'Not the same colour,' Tessa said with a shake of her head. 'Green, a beautiful bright green. He was very polite as I remember and gave me a large tip when he left.'

'Ah, well, that says it all, of course, if he gave you a large tip.' Tessa swiped over her shoulder at her husband.

'Be quiet, you.'

'Is that enough to tickle your interest, Fran?' Martin chuckled.

The lads were coming in now and Frances moved off silently to help serve the dinners.

In her room later that night, Frances pulled an old-fashioned trunk out from beneath the washstand. It hadn't been opened in the six years she had been here and was covered in dust. Grabbing an old cardigan, she wiped the top then opened the lid. This was all that was left of her past—a photograph of her parents before their divorce when she was seven; her grandmother's china tea service wrapped in tissue paper and packed in a cardboard box; a couple of empty silver photo frames; a pair of china parrots; an autograph book from schooldays and a plastic bag full of plaits of horse hair from all the horses she had ever looked after.

She sat back on her heels and thought about the strict disciplinarian who had been her grandmother, overruling every wish of Frances in the name of doing right by her. To this end she had been educated to a fitting standard and fitted for a suitable position in life.

The training had been a secretarial one and the position in a stuffy country solicitor's office, a job she had hated. Within a week of her grandmother's funeral, Frances had thrown caution to the winds and sold their home and resigned from her job.

She smiled to herself as she remembered the exhilaration of those first heady days of freedom. After many months of rejections from trainers who told her she was too inexperienced to be a jockey or who were brazenly sexist in their rejection, when her savings were sinking fast and she feared defeat, Martin Truscott had opened the door for her.

The rest was a real success story and she had repaid Martin's faith in her one hundred fold until a day at Lingfield sixteen months ago. They had been bunched up tight on the rails before the home straight when a drunken man made a dash across the course for a bet. The first Frances knew of fear was when the horse and jockey immediately in front of her disappeared. She threw her weight back in the saddle as the cry of the jockey behind her rang in her ears.

Her mount's hindquarters were bunched to jump but his front feet were knocked from under him by the bulk of the fallen horse. The voice through the Tannoy remained with her, though everything else collapsed around her. It was four pain-filled weeks before she knew exactly what had happened.

*   *   *

The following Saturday, Frances stood beside Tessa in Manchester Airport. Martin joined them and pushed some magazines into her hand luggage.

'I feel such a fool.' Frances turned to Tessa. 'Here I am, twenty-five years old, and a bag of nerves because I've never flown before.'

'Once you're in the departure lounge it's just a matter of following the herd,' Martin said with the confidence of one who had flown all over the world. 'Watch for your gate number on the monitor and you'll be fine.'

'You'll be met?' Tessa checked anxiously.

'Yes. The man at the bank asked for my arrival time and said he would fax it out to Mr Harding.'

'Good. Well, let's hear from you as soon as you get settled.'

There were tears in her eyes and Frances leaned forward to hug her.

'I will, and look after yourself,' she called as Martin chiwied her towards the departure lounge.

One last hug and an assurance that there was always a place for her with them should she need it, and then there was no turning back.

CHAPTER TWO

Five hours later, Frances was beginning to wonder if she and Kane Harding were destined never to meet. Most of her fellow travellers had already left the building and the Tannoy was announcing in Spanish the arrival of the next flight. Once more she allowed her eyes to wander over every person in sight.

No-one seemed the least bit interested in her. The loudspeaker fell silent and Frances chewed at her lip as the first feelings of panic gurgled in her stomach. She considered whether or not to take a taxi as, after all, she did have the address of her destination.

The Tannoy rasped, then came to life again, this time with an English voice, asking for a Mr Francis Gardiner to go to the information desk, please. Frances was horrified. Did this mean her new employer was expecting a man or had they just mixed their facts at the desk? With her heart in her mouth, she pushed her luggage trolley in the direction of the information desk.

There was a uniformed person talking to the girl behind the desk. At the end of the counter was a group of three men. The short, fat one was gesticulating wildly with both hands, while the taller of the group appeared to be in an extremely bad temper about something.

Frances waited patiently by the desk until the girl detached herself from the official who then turned to the couple behind him. The girl frowned when Frances told her who she was and asked to see her passport. After studying it carefully, she waved it in the direction of the group standing at the far end of the counter and called to them in Spanish.

The tall, angry one questioned the girl in her own language then turned to Frances.

'You say you are Frances Gardiner?'

Frances struggled to reply for there was no doubting who this man was for the green eyes blazing down into her own could only be those of Kane Harding. Battling for the control of her emotions and on the point of hysteria, Frances managed a cool, 'I am.'

'Then I'm afraid there has been a mistake and you will have to catch the next flight back.'

Frances gasped.

'I b-beg your pardon?'

'I think you heard me.'

'I did, but I find it hard to believe I heard right.'

'Then I suggest, Ms Gardiner, you try a little harder,' he snapped and made to walk away.

'You didn't stipulate the gender of the secretary in your advert,' she called after him.

10

Swinging round to face her he said, 'You can't do that these days, didn't you know? It's called sexual discrimination.'

'That's exactly what this is. I can do this job as well as any man, probably better, and the only reason you have for not giving me a chance is because I'm a woman. If that is not discrimination I don't know what is and I'll shout it to every riding magazine that will listen.'

'Why, you . . .'

Frances thought she was about to be attacked there and then in the airport terminal. She ducked instinctively then felt a large hand grab the shoulder of her jacket. Sweeping her off her feet like a wayward child, she was hustled outside.

Concentrating all her efforts on trying to release herself from the undignified position she was in she failed to notice that another plane load of passengers was disembarking.

'Unless you want to make a scene in front of all these people,' he said, drawing her attention to the swelling crowd behind them, 'I suggest we hold this conversation somewhere more fitting.'

A white four-wheel-drive vehicle stood in the carpark, with *Harding Ranch* emblazoned in brown scroll across its door panels. He opened the passenger door for her and threw her case into the back before climbing in and starting the engine.

'Where are we going?'

She was anxious not to get stranded somewhere where it might be difficult for her to find her own way back to the airport.

'To the ranch, where else,' he snapped. 'In case you hadn't noticed, it's getting quite late, thanks to your fooling around back there. And while I am sure a night in the airport wouldn't do you any harm, you can stay at the ranch instead and we can carry on our discussion in comfort.'

Frances tried to ignore him. At least she was to have a bed for the night. The dark had swept down unnoticed, Frances realised, as she tried to see something of the countryside they were passing through. They were on a wide, well-made road that was carrying them north through chains of hills. Now and again they would pass through small villages of flat-roofed, shuttered houses clustered by the roadside.

It was over an hour since she'd landed, and Frances's stomach was rumbling with hunger as he spoke again.

'It won't be long now. We are climbing into the hills and the ranch lies in a valley on the other side, just north of La Laguna.'

Tall trees closed around them, darkening the interior of the car. The road began to wind and the sound of the car's engine changed as it pulled up a hill.

'Do you have family at the ranch?'

She sneaked a glance at the dark profile of his head barely discernible in the light of the dashboard.

'No, I live alone.'

'Are there any other women at the ranch?' Frances tried to sound nonchalant, failed and swallowed hard.

Turning his head momentarily, the green eyes flashed out through the darkness.

'Are you afraid I may seduce you before I set you free, Ms Gardiner?' Frances felt ridiculous.

'No, of course not. I was just curious about the place, that's all. I have never been abroad before. I was looking forward to this job very much.'

Liar, she accused herself, you'd much rather be back at Martin's and Tessa's settling the horses for the night.

'Well, that's a pity because it is essential I have a man for the job.'

'Why?'

His voice was hard when he spoke.

'Because men can separate business from pleasure. Women seem unable to grasp even the rudiments of this separation. I refuse to have my working life interrupted and messed about by silly females who dress up and prance around believing you should take notice of them and go into sulks when you don't. When they consider a cup of coffee more important than a telephone message, then they are no use to me.'

Frances gazed back at her reflection in the darkened window, embarrassed by the vehemence in his statement.

The road dipped down now and across the darkness lights were winking in the valley below them. She was dying to ask more questions about the place but wisely decided to hold her peace. In silence they approached the ranch. Lights flooded from the front door at the sound of their vehicle. It was too dark to see much but Frances got the impression of a long, low building with a verandah running the entire length. The heavily-carved door was flung back and a small bird-like figure all in black called out in Spanish to Kane.

He answered her in the same language as he swung Frances's case from the vehicle. There came an explosion of laughter from the tiny woman on the steps as she flung her hands up to her face then clasped them tightly in front of her flat chest.

'Connie will show you to your room,' he snapped to Frances, a deep scowl between his brows. 'I will see you in my office after dinner.'

Barely giving her time to ease the stiffness from her limbs, he climbed back into the Jeep, revved the engine and was away before she could ask where his office was.

'Please, senorita, to come.'

The small woman was beckoning her to

enter the house, so she picked up her case and, mounting the two steps, crossed the verandah to the front door.

'Connie,' she asked hesitantly.

'Si, Coney.'

Frances smiled at the pronunciation wondering who on earth had first called her by that name for it obviously wasn't her real name.

The hall was beautiful with its polished wood floor and curving staircase. Roughcast white walls were hung on two sides with full-length tapestries whose aged colours still drew the eye to their unfolding stories. Wall lights in wrought-iron brackets stood out against smutty shadows and in the large hall itself there were only three pieces of furniture, two heavy, ornately-carved, tall-backed chairs and a massive box, much scored, with metal handles on each end.

Halfway up the stairs they met a young man coming down who smiled shyly and murmured, 'Good evening.' On the point of asking Connie who the person was, an elderly couple passed them on the head of the stairs, bowing an acknowledgement as they passed. Frances's step lightened. So it was more like a hotel than a private house.

Connie showed Frances into a bedroom whose only concession to colour was the blue of the curtains that edged the shuttered windows and the spread on the double bed.

The furniture was all dark wood and the walls a continuation of the white roughcast of the lower hall. A large, framed portrait of a woman in a blue velvet gown whose tight lacing denied her any figure and whose hair was confined to a snood looked down on them with cold hostility.

Frances shivered.

'Dinner is at nine, si,' Connie said and held up nine fingers.

Frances smiled wondering what the little woman did for twelve o'clock! Nodding her understanding, Frances thanked Connie and closed the door softly behind her. Alone at last and so tired. Ignoring her luggage, she flung herself on to the bed and stared at the ceiling. How on earth was she going to convince that stupid man that she must be allowed to stay? For stay she must—the very thought of turning up on Martin's doorstep so soon was just not on.

She jumped when she realised she was falling asleep. Rolling from the bed, she stretched her arms and back gently, then flung open her suitcase and sorted through for something to wear for dinner. The people she had seen on the stairs were well dressed.

She rummaged for a while then picked out a midnight-blue crinkle silk dress that she had splashed out for when she had been invited to an owners' party after a particularly successful win two years ago. Might as well try to make a good impression.

The bathroom was basic but satisfactory, with a plentiful supply of thick white towels and lots of hot water. After her shower, Frances dressed carefully, applying what little make-up she possessed. She decided to put her hair up in a complicated chignon that would hopefully add a little sophistication and help her already flagging confidence.

Her watch allowed her exactly eight minutes to find the dining-room as she twirled in front of the cheval mirror, quite liking what she saw. The tight, sleeveless bodice of the dress defined her figure, usually swamped by the blouses and shirts she wore.

Satisfied that she had done her best with her appearance, she left the room and went in search of the other guests. There must have been twenty people or more in the large room, whose double doors leading from the hall stood wide open, when Frances entered. There was a bar to the right of the doors and Frances had just picked up a small sherry when a booming noise fit to challenge the breaking of the sound barrier split across her ears nearly making her spill her drink.

A warm chuckle close to her left ear made her swing round and match glances with a pair of laughing blue eyes in a rather ugly face with panhandle ears.

'It is a bit much, senorita, but you get used to it.'

Frances smiled back.

'Is that the dinner gong?'

'Si. May I escort you in to dinner?'

He made a beautiful bow and offered her his arm.

'Why, thank you, sir.'

They were laughing as they followed the others into a long, refectory-like room whose wails were hung with an assortment of armoury and weapons from bygone days. People were seating themselves at the long, central table and Frances felt that the only things missing were the reeds on the floor and the dogs roaming around waiting for bones!

The man, who had introduced himself as Gilbert de Sousa, found them places at the table and began explaining a little of the history of the ranch.

'The first stones of the original house that stood here were believed to have been laid at the beginning of the sixteenth century by a Spanish conqueror in the army of Fernandez de Lugo when they took the island from the Guanches, the original natives of Tenerife. The house as you see it today was completed in eighteen-twenty-three by a Frenchman who had been a very successful pirate and was rewarded by the Spanish after giving help in the battle against Nelson in seventeen-ninety-seven. This was the battle in which your Lord Nelson lost his arm.'

He gave her a wicked chuckle.

'The Frenchman had many children from many wives, but one wife belonged to the Guanche people and she gave birth to a strong son. This son took and held the ranch for his own. The present owner is a direct descendant.'

Gilbert was talkative and friendly and Frances decided that now might be a good time to put her own predicament before him.

They had returned to the lounge with their coffee when Gilbert was called away to the telephone. Connie appeared beside the arm of Frances's chair. 'I take you to the senor now, si?'

It sounded like a request but Frances wasn't fooled for a second. This was an order.

Putting on a winning smile she said, 'Si,' and following Connie's lead went through a doorway at the rear of the hall and across a paved patio lit by heavy, old lanterns.

The office, she noted when she entered it, was a maelstrom of modern technology. Amongst the mess sat the tall figure of Kane Harding, a deep frown scoring his brow and a twitch tweaking along his jawbone. Connie had disappeared.

'Take a seat, Ms Gardiner. I hope your accommodation is to your liking.'

He sounded as though he couldn't care less whether she was comfortable or not, so she didn't bother to answer. Instead, as a basically

19

tidy person herself, she was horrified to see such chaos when with so much expensive machinery around it was totally unnecessary.

'Why is there such a mess? Have you been burgled or something?'

'No. We have not been burgled, Ms Gardiner. This is not England. The office is in this mess, as you call it, because my secretaries were more interested in painting their nails than attending to their work.'

His voice was full of anger.

'Didn't anyone check them out for you?'

'I'm a busy man.' He spoke clearly and slowly as though to a child. 'When I hire someone to do a job I expect them to do it.'

'And you want a man to come and sort this out?' She could not keep the surprise out of her voice.

'What is so strange about that?'

'Well, considering what percentage of women in the world today are tidying up after men I would hazard a guess that your chances of getting a man to tidy this lot up were pretty thin. No wonder you didn't take up my references. Martin said you were snatching at straws.'

'Well, I certainly got the short end with you, didn't I?'

If anyone had told Frances an hour ago that she would be standing here arguing with this man, she would not have believed them. Now he stood up and Frances gulped, suddenly aware of what she had done. The green eyes had narrowed and turned dangerously still. Frances was frozen as his gaze dropped slowly down the length of her body and back to her hair.

'You took a lot of trouble dressing tonight. I wonder why.'

Frances's face burned at the innuendo.

Through gritted teeth she said, 'I wish you luck with all your mess here, Mr Harding.'

She rose from the chair to make a grand exit but his hand on her upper arm jerked her back. His eyes glittered with gem-like hardness as he spoke. 'Do you have a man at home?'

'That is none of . . .'

'Do you?' he asked again.

Frances could feel herself pale with fright.

'No, I do not if it is any of . . .'

'Then who is this Martin you refer to?'

'My employer.'

'Will he give you a reference?'

'Yes.'

'Why did you leave to apply for this job?'

'I'd been ill. I needed a change.'

His hand dropped from her arm.

'Give me a number for this Martin, who, Martin?'

'Truscott, Martin Truscott.'

Frances proceeded to give out the number of the racing stables then hovered in the background. He gave her a pointed look then signalled that she should leave the room, before turning back to the telephone on the desk.

Frances sat on the tiled edge that surrounded the fountain. The moon shone through the leaves of the trees that grew in the patio, casting moving shadows over the mosaic floor. A gentle breeze rocked the tips of the trees as they brushed the overhanging wooden balconies of the upper rooms. She was confident that Martin would give her the necessary references but to what extent would they influence this dreadful man's decision about her future? Knowing she still wanted the job despite the unpleasantness of her possible employer gave the waiting a touch of desperation.

Trailing her fingers through the water, a stately goldfish rubbed its belly over them. She was delighted at this gesture but try as she would the fish refused to repeat the pleasure.

Thanks to Gilbert de Sousa, she now knew that the ranch consisted of a stud, where Kane bred horses for three-day eventing, a school, for horsemasters, who came from all over the world to train and learn the Harding way to success. The people she had met in the house were those horsemasters and would stay for periods of six weeks at a time. Gilbert was the chief instructor at the school.

From Gilbert she had also learned that Kane had his own house and stables on the far side of the ranch where he worked out with his horses between shows. So all things considered, his absence when he was competing, his distance from the office when he was home and the fact that he expected his secretary to work on their own initiative, the job was looking more attractive by the minute. She was convinced she could keep it if only he would give her the chance.

When she looked up, he was standing in the open doorway of the office, watching her. He walked towards her, hands pushed down in his trouser pockets.

'I'm going to Brazil tomorrow. If you can have this mess tidied up by the time I return, the job is yours.'

'Right.'

He was on his way back to the office when he stopped and turned. 'What illness did you say you were recovering from?'

Frances's heart missed a beat, then did a mad tattoo.

'Pneumonia. The English weather, you know. I needed a change of climate.'

It sounded ridiculous.

'How long will you be gone?' she asked, trying to distract him. It worked.

'Five, possibly six days, quite long enough for you to prove yourself here, Ms Gardiner.'

Throwing the comments over his shoulder, he entered the office and shut the door with a heavy thud.

Beaming like a Cheshire cat, Frances made her way back through the house and up to her room. She would astound him with her efficiency upon his return and the job would be hers.

CHAPTER THREE

In the cold light of morning and having woken to grey skies and a miserable drizzle, the feelings of last night's euphoria had curled up and died. Too late for breakfast and reluctant to seek out Connie and ask for coffee and toast, Frances now stood in the chilly office and surveyed the task before her. With a sigh she sat down at the desk she had seen Kane occupy the night before and glanced through some of the documentation that littered the top.

There were breeding charts, calendars, work schedules and holiday rosters to pin up on the wall; the computer, printer and keyboard were all stacked on top of one another and pushed back into a corner; a fax machine had run out of paper and a photocopier that Frances was sure would give out a messy copy. On the floor were two overflowing wastebins and a crisscross of wires to trip over.

By lunch time, the papers on the desk top had been sorted into separate piles, the paper bins emptied and the wires re-routed to safer positions. The fax machine was once more ready for use and the photocopier, as though to lighten Frances's depression, had given out a perfect copy.

The rain had stopped and the clouds disappeared and the only sound coming through the open door was the water tinkling in the fountain.

Gilbert was at the lunch table when she arrived and left off talking to his neighbour to signal to Frances there was an empty seat on his other side.

'So you are to stay with us, good.'

He smiled as he pulled out the seat for her.

'Please may I introduce you to Prudence Baker, another instructor at the school. Prudence,' he said turning to the woman on the right, 'this is Senorita Frances Gardiner, who our good boss thought was a man.'

His face crinkled with laughter, and Prudence smiled sympathetically.

'Please call me Pru, everyone else does. That must have been some meeting at the airport when his lordship discovered he'd hired yet another female. I'm surprised you got this far.'

Later, as they sat on the verandah drinking their coffee and waiting for Gilbert to join them, Pru explained that she wasn't needed again until three when the afternoon school started.

'Nothing moves around here in the heat of the day.'

'You must see it all before you can hope to understand the business,' Gilbert insisted as he came out to join them, 'and you must meet

26

all the staff. It is all very well meeting the horsemasters but they come and go. Most of the staff have been here for many years. Some were even born here on the ranch. Do you ride?'

'Sorry.'

The spontaneous lie startled her. Where had it come from, then, oh, well, she was there as a secretary. There was no need to admit to being a jockey. That would really put them off.

'A great pity, senorita. It is the best way to see the ranch.'

'Please, call me Fran, all my friends at home do.'

Half an hour later, they took an open-topped Jeep and she was grateful she had taken time to change into shorts and shirt and plait her long hair. The sun was very hot still and Gilbert made her wear a flat-topped hat with a wide brim. The whole ranch took on a magical quality as they left the white-washed buildings behind and headed up a steep hillside track.

The great Mount Teide floated on a cloud before them as they breasted the hill. Frances gasped at the illusion for in fact the mountain was in the far distance, at the centre of the island. Gilbert turned the Jeep so that they were facing back the way they had come and now the view changed again and they were gazing down into the valley of Aguere.

'From here you can see the whole ranch.'
Gilbert began to point out the buildings. There was the main house with its white walls and red-tiled roof, three barns of stabling, two riding schools, a well-laid-out cross-country course, a jumping paddock and a training run. On the far side of the valley there was a citrus orchard and grazing, another stable block and a house.

'Is that Mr Harding's house?' she asked.

'No, they belong to the stud. Senor Kane's home is behind those trees on your right.'

They returned to the property and Frances was introduced to Julio Perez, the stud groom, also Eduardo Vives Salvador and Maurice Beckworth, both of whom were instructors under Gilbert. Grooms too numerous to remember also appeared though Gilbert did assure her she would get to know them all in time.

She discovered in the days that followed that she was to be the co-ordinator of all the differing aspects of the ranch. Gilbert, Julio and Connie all brought their financial accounts, time schedules, and numerous problems to her office and three out of the next five evenings were spent working very late.

It came as quite a shock when she woke one morning and discovered it was Saturday, the day Kane Harding was due home and the day she would find out whether or not she had a

28

permanent job.

Mist and drizzle hung around until mid morning and Frances hoped it wasn't an omen for her meeting with Kane Harding. She swiped the duster over the cleared surface of the desk for the hundredth time. The backlog of work had been sorted, dealt with, filed and keyed into the computer. Walls were now bare of all but the two prints she had picked up at La Laguna when Gilbert had taken her for a look around the town.

Connie had seen the prints and insisted that her grandson would frame them for her, so the pictures now hung in beautiful pine frames, Frances's pride and joy along with her newly-acquired miniature rose and a broad, glossy-leafed plant that looked as though it might well reach the ceiling some day.

Her watch showed twelve-fifty-five so Harding or no Harding she was going to go to lunch. She had adapted well to the new lifestyle, rising early and working through until one o'clock, then resting through the early afternoon before starting work again at three.

The evening meal wasn't until nine and Frances had been working right up until the last minute, giving herself just enough time to shower and change. Gilbert had noticed and objected, telling her that the other secretaries had all finished at six.

Now, as she stood in front of the dressing-table mirror in her room and rolled up the long plait of hair, pinning it to the top of her head, she looked at the newly-emerging cheeks instead of hollows and the faint blush of tan that had replaced the drawn white look she had arrived with. The blue linen dress was belted in to her tiny waist and she shook the folds of the skirt to discourage any creasing.

Well, Mr Harding, she thought, as she fastened her small locket at her throat, I have done my best and if it is not good enough for you, then you deserve what you get in my place.

With a last look in the mirror, she slipped her feet back into the blue sandals, tucked a handkerchief beneath her watch strap and with head high went down to lunch. One or two people greeted her as she sat down then all eyes turned to the doorway as Kane Harding arrived with a group of people.

Frances caught her breath. He certainly didn't look like the same man she remembered from the previous week. He dominated the room at that moment with the casual ease of accustomed acclaim and was without doubt the most attractive man she had ever seen. His height gave him advantage over his company and he scanned the room quickly as he listened to what they had to say. His glance locked momentarily on Frances then his full attention was given to the woman by his side.

Dark, overlong hair was smoothed back from his face allowing Frances a good view of fine bone structure from sloping cheekbones to long straight nose. The mouth was twisted into tight attention above a clean firm jaw line and Frances couldn't help wonder what difference it would make should he relax and pull that mouth back in a smile.

After lunch, she made a hasty exit. Normally she would spend the siesta in some shady part of the garden, but today a restlessness gripped her and she decided to walk down to the stables. She had made the rounds of the barns with Gilbert but never made the time to become acquainted with the horses there.

As she wandered along the rows of stalls giving a pat and a quiet word to any head she found hanging over the door, she became aware of voices behind her. Not wanting to be caught and thought to be disturbing the horses' rest period, she ducked into the next available space and found herself in the hay shed.

'I just know you are the only person who can help me. Please, Kane darling, I want him ready for Munich.'

The voice pleaded very prettily, Frances thought, and there was no question who the man was.

'I'm sorry, Pilar. You know my feelings on the matter. The horse is too green, too flighty.'

'You are just angry with me because I bought him without your approval. He is fast, supple and obedient. What more could you ask for?'

'He drops his legs over the jumps and he has yet to learn to concentrate in the dressage arena.'

'But you can teach him these things.'

'Not unless he wants to learn and I have yet to be convinced that he does.'

The woman's voice took on a hard petulance.

'Then I shall get Drago to train him. He can do anything with a horse.'

'Including spoiling him.'

Frances could almost hear the woman shrug.

'He gets results, even if his methods are not your own.'

There was a long silence and Frances wondered if they had moved on. Then Kane spoke again with a heavy voice.

'All right, Pilar, bring him over, but I'm making no promises.'

'You never do, darling,' the woman purred.

Frances could feel the heat run up her face as she realised the pair had probably been kissing. They were walking away now and Frances let go a sigh of relief. It would have been too awful if they had moved into the hay shed and found her eavesdropping on their conversation.

She was back in the office on the dot of three when Kane walked in and shut the door behind him. Her heart leaped into her throat and she knew exactly how it would feel to be shut in a tiger's cage.

He was dressed in a yellow sports shirt and beige slacks. His golden tan below the short sleeves and above the open neck of the shirt added to the tiger image which was total when you let yourself look, as Francis did now, into those startling eyes.

'Ms Gardiner,' he began.

'Mr Harding.'

'I see you have made yourself at home.'

'Well, whatever I have done it must be an improvement on what it was.'

'Quite. I'm pleased to see you made it back from the stables in time for our meeting.'

Frances felt all the wind rush from her body. With trembling legs she struggled to hold an outward composure.

'I wasn't aware we had a meeting scheduled.'

He surveyed the room, taking in her pictures with raised eyebrows. Then his gaze switched back to her face, giving it a hard, thoughtful stare. 'I want the livery accommodation listing for the next six weeks.' Frances dropped her chin.

'Certainly. If you will just acknowledge those requests and sign the cheques, I"Il have the listings in a moment.'

He sat down at the opposite desk and with a swiftness she deplored, he scrawled over everything and came to stand behind her. She accessed the file she needed on the computer, keyed in her request and waited while the printer reeled out the relevant list. When she turned around to hand it to him, he was smiling.

'The job is yours, Ms Gardiner.'

'Fran.'

He nodded his acknowledgement.

'You had better call me Kane. Everyone else does.'

Handing back the list he said, 'See if you can fit in one more livery. The name is Firefly, the owner Senora Mendoza.'

Startled, Frances repeated the horse's name.

'Firefly.'

'You have heard of him?' he asked with a frown.

'Not this one, no. The horse I knew was . . .'

She pulled herself up just in time. She had nearly said he had been a racer.

'He was one at the local riding school. It must be a popular name for a horse, don't you think?

Oh, no! She was babbling.

'You ride?'

'No, yes, well, I did as a child, but I don't any more.'

'Why not?'

Frances wished she was dead. This was getting worse by the minute. Stick to the truth, an inner voice was warning. Trim its edges but stick to the truth.

'I had an accident. It scared me and I haven't ridden since.'

'That's a shame. You must let someone help you get back into the saddle while you are here,' he said, but it was obvious he had lost interest. 'I will be over tomorrow morning to bring you up to date and answer any queries you may have and then you will be on your own. Here's my phone connection. Give me a ring anytime you feel you don't have the authority to deal with something.'

He let his gaze slide once more around the office.

'Good,' he added. 'Keep your personal life free of entanglements and you'll do fine.'

He smiled once more and left.

CHAPTER FOUR

Patronising oaf, Frances fumed, deciding that his smile had done nothing for him after all. Chewing her lip she wondered about the other bit of information that had surprised her.

Firefly had been a horse in Martin's stable at the time of her accident. In fact he had belonged to the same couple who had owned her ride, Midnight Express. The Gregory family had been very kind, insisting that no blame be attached to either stable or jockey when Express was destroyed. It had taken its toll of their enthusiasm for the sport, however, and Firefly had been sold The three-year-old had been full of racing promise, so this couldn't be the same horse, yet just the name had made her jump. At the time, friends had flooded her with promises of work on her return from the hospital but the doctors warnings had stayed with her. Riding, certainly racing, was extremely doubtful. Her arms would never be strong enough to control a racing horse again.

Her love of horses had started early with twice-weekly rides at a local stable. When there had been no-one to hold and comfort a small girl she had taken her problems to a favourite pony. He listened patiently, never criticised and provided all the warmth her grandmother could not. Frances never questioned if this love could not be found with another human being.

She had lived for the past six years in close company, with the shared love of her friends, Martin and Tessa, and had listened and commiserated with the other lads on their love affairs and marriage problems. Men had asked her out on dates and a very wealthy owner had once proposed to her. But no relationship ever provided the surge of adrenaline she got when the ground was flashing beneath her, the fear, the excitement, the flood of success that filled the heart near to bursting when she passed the winning post.

No relationship had given her the courage to stand alone in a man's world, to swallow the tears when she had broken bones, or failed to bring a horse up to scratch. Animals gave their trust and their love unstintingly. No human being Frances had ever known had done that.

That evening, she left the office at six. She had promised to go and watch Gilbert's last lesson of the day at seven and wanted to have a shower and change her clothes before that. Gilbert was fast becoming a good friend with a cheeky sense of humour. Tonight he wanted her to see another side of his work, for he was devoted to his job.

It was a private lesson, a young man who lived locally and in whom Gilbert had seen great potential. The young man was poor but all his money went into saving for the occasional lesson with Gilbert.

'I'd love to come,' she had confirmed when they had been sitting out on the verandah with drinks the previous evening.

'Perhaps when you see how gentle I am you will let me teach you to ride again.'

Frances had laughed.

'You mean, you don't chase your students around the school shouting, heels down, hands still, head up!'

'No, no, I am much more subtle. I tell them to keep their derrière in the saddle.'

Tonight was cooler so she let down her hair and wore a finely-pleated skirt with a matching close-fitting jumper. When she was dressed to her satisfaction, she thrust her feet into brown loafers, grabbed a lightweight jacket from the chair by the door and trotted lightly down the stairs and out on to the verandah.

Here she hurtled headlong into Senora Mendoza. The woman stepped back with a small scream and sank her stiletto heel into the top of Kane Harding's foot.

'You clumsy girl. Why don't you watch where you're going!' she screeched at Frances.

Kane was rubbing his injured foot up and down the calf of his other leg, the bright green eyes fixed on Frances.

'I'm sorry, I didn't realise.'

Pru was giving her a sympathetic thumbs-up

38

from the sidelines.

'Realise what, you stupid girl?' then she let out another shriek as she saw that the narrow heel was dangling from the shoe.

'Come along, Pilar. José will mend your shoe. I'll see you in the office in the morning, Frances,' Kane snapped.

With a nod of her head, she acknowledged his rebuke then with a wave to Pru, ran down the steps and followed the gravel pathway to the second school standing some one and a half miles from the main house, where Gilbert was working with his pupil.

The boy was good. Though she had little knowledge of either show jumping or dressage, she could recognise a promising rider. His natural empathy with his mount and its willingness to follow his commands made the oneness of their movements beautiful to watch.

Gilbert was taking the boy through basic work, crossing and re-crossing the school, changing the horse's leading stride and rhythm again and again. After a while, to Gilbert's quiet command and with no outward sign on the boy's part, the horse began to undertake more complicated movements. Frances was enthralled.

Never in her life had she seen a man and a horse combine to such effect. Oh, racing was beautiful and a good combination of horse and jockey could create a fantastic power. But it was a wild power, a surge of natural energy. What was happening here before her was something totally different.

At the end of the lesson Frances climbed down from the viewing gallery and waited patiently for Gilbert and his student to come out of the great double doors of the school. The horse was a grey stallion and he came out full of his own importance. A groom took the horse off to his stable. Gilbert touched the boy on the arm and led him over to where Frances stood.

'Fran, I would like you to meet Juan Carlos Lopez. Juan, Senorita Frances Gardiner.'

The young man swept off his hat and bowed over her hand.

'It's good to meet with you, Senorita Gardiner.'

'I was very impressed with your riding, senor.'

'Thank you.'

He moved around restlessly, as though in a hurry to leave, his eyes flickering from left to right.

Gilbert frowned, then giving the boy his monkey grin said, 'It's time to go.'

'Goodbye, senor, senorita.'

He left them, his long legs carrying him like a fleeting shadow across the stones.

'He's in a hurry,' Frances remarked.

'He is not welcome here. He knows this and does not like to linger.'

'I don't understand.'

Gilbert tucked her arm under his and began to lead her back towards the house.

'No, you should not understand. It is not for us to worry about.'

It was still early for dinner so Frances went into the lounge for a drink while Gilbert went off in search of Connie. Pru was sitting with Eduardo and Maurice on the far side of the room and beckoned Frances to join them. Eduardo, was very Spanish, with stilted English and impeccable manners. He stood immediately to let Frances sit down before pushing another chair forward into their group. Maurice Beckworth, on the other hand, was a North country Englishman who was sprawled in his chair, and merely lifted a hand in greeting.

'Well, you've certainly managed to endear yourself to our Pilar,' he said, followed by a warm chuckle.

Frances grinned back.

'What happened?'

'Oh, the shoe wouldn't mend and his lordship whisked her away to his castle for a spot of magic,' Pru replied.

'You say the stupidest things, Pru,' Maurice growled from the depths of his chair.

Pru made a face at him before asking Frances, 'So how's your working relationship with his lordship progressing?'

'I'm a permanent fixture, if that's what

41

you mean,' Frances replied, beaming from ear to ear.

'Good for you, girl. I never would have believed he would hire another woman. They all fell for him, you know. Tried every trick in the book to catch his attention. One of them went so far as to stow away in the horsebox when he went to Spain. She dragged around the course after him, making a fuss of the horses, flinging her arms around his neck when he was presented with a cup and getting herself in the papers. Then to crown it all, she swooped half-naked into a picture a passerby was taking as Kane was stripped to the waist washing down after the cross country. He was livid apparently but not half as mad as when he realised she had got hold of the photograph and sold it to the papers after he had fired her, woman scorned and all that.'

'Good grief! Where did he find these women in the first place?'

'Perfectly respectable agencies. Not the agencies fault if our delectable boss sends them stir crazy.'

'Where does Pilar Mendoza fit into all this then?'

Pru looked thoughtful and pursed her lips.

'Well, she's the official brand and a bit of a problem. While her main function is to keep our lordship happy in a more personal way, shall we say, she's a bit of a snoop. The boss doesn't like it so she tends to keep it under

42

wraps, so be careful how you treat her and be wary if you find her in your office.'

At that moment, Kane and Pilar entered the lounge and were rapidly engulfed by eager horsemasters, all wanting, Pru said, to consult the lord and master as to their particular needs.

'Pathetic, really, some of them.'

'That's a bit thick, Pru,' Maurice objected.

'I am with Pru, si,' Eduardo agreed.

'I saw a wonderful young student tonight,' Frances burst out. 'He and the horse worked like a dream.'

The company around her fell silent and looked decidedly uncomfortable. It wasn't until Gilbert's hand fell gently on to her shoulder that she realised her mistake. He had said that the young Juan wasn't welcome on the ranch.

She smiled with relief when Gilbert suggested that they join an elderly couple Gilbert was tutoring. The wife had broken her hip in an accident. Frances's sympathy went out to the woman who had ridden all of her life and was determined not to let the injury put an end to her riding.

As she accompanied Gilbert in to dinner, she remarked on the woman's courage and was shocked when he not only disagreed with her but condemned people who didn't know when to let go. They were in the middle of a heated debate when Kane spoke from behind them.

'I'm pleased to see it's not only me she shouts at. A word, Frances.'

His hand was on her arm, lifting her away from the table before Gilbert could open his mouth. They moved out of the dining-room and into the hall. 'I wish you would call me Fran. I dislike the awkwardness of my full name.'

'Perhaps you would prefer Frank.'

Frances decided to ignore that remark.

'What can I do for you? I'm going to be late at the table.'

'It will still be there when I have finished with you.'

Frances didn't like the sound of that.

'Is something wrong?'

The green eyes narrowed and the twitching was back along his jaw. 'With your work, no. I would like you to mingle more with the horsemasters.'

'Mingle?'

Frances was beginning to understand the chemistry that had driven his previous secretaries slightly mad. Just as well I'm immune, she thought. 'Mingle? I don't understand.'

'I would also like you to play hostess at a dinner I'm giving a week from today. I would have told you in the morning but I'm afraid I won't be able to make our meeting now. My day is fully booked.'

'I see, well, if it's part of the job I can hardly refuse.'

'Do you wish to refuse?'

'No, I don't think I do.'

'Good. Then perhaps in future, instead of avoiding me when I come into meals, you will join me in circulating with the horsemasters.'

Heavens, was she to have no time to herself at all? She opened her mouth to complain, then stopped herself. Orders didn't require replies. She looked up and caught him watching her. Neither spoke as he continued to explore her face with his cold stare.

France's eyes flickered nervously from side to side, then down to the ground and back up again. Shivers were running up and down her spine and spreading out to form goose bumps on her arms. She rubbed them automatically.

'If that's all, l"II get back to my meal.'

'Of course. Until tomorrow evening then.'

'No please or thank you from him, just orders,' she told her friends when she was back at the table. 'You will join me in circulating with the horsemasters,' she mimicked Kane's voice making Gilbert and Pru laugh.

'Never mind,' Pru said with an accompanying prod in the ribs. Just think of all that money mounting up in the bank. You'll be wining and dining with some of the richest people in the world.'

Frances wanted to say that she had been

45

there, for she had been very popular with the owners although she had not been impressed with the trappings of wealth, or the people who wore them.

*   *   *

Frances continued to follow young Juan Carlos's progress until one day she arrived at the school to hear voices raised in argument. There was no mistaking the sharp, bitter tones of Pilar Mendoza.

'You will be finished here when Kane hears of this.'

'The school is my domain, senora. I say whom I teach and whom I do not. The senor knows this. Juan Carlos Lopez is a pupil under my tuition and he pays like everyone else.'

'But he is not everyone else, is he? He has been forbidden on the ranch, you know this and yet you go against your employer's wishes.'

The tall dark figure of Juan Carlos stood in a nearby stable staring at Frances. He must hear them, she thought. Why doesn't he leave? She made to join him but changed her mind and walked towards the open doors of the school.

Pilar was dressed for riding, her whip twitching like the tail of an angry cat.

Gilbert was standing his ground.

'This matter is between myself and the

46

senor, senora, and no-one else. Ah, Senorita Frances, you have come to find me, si?'

Pilar turned her head as Frances came through the open doors. 'What are you doing down here?' she snapped.

Frances nodded her head in greeting and said, 'I work here.'

Without another word, the Spanish woman turned her back on them and stalked away.

'She will make trouble for you,' Frances spoke quietly.

'She will try,' Gilbert agreed, an expression of pain stamped on his face. 'The boy is outside in the stable.'

'Si, I know, he waits for me. We must make other arrangements. It is important that he continues his instruction.'

'What has he done to make Kane ban him from the ranch?'

'Ah, Fran, it is a long story.'

He took hold of her hand and pulled it through his arm.

'A story which only Kane can tell.'

They left the school together, and Juan Carlos came across the yard to meet them. Then he and Gilbert climbed into the Jeep and drove away.

Frances returned to the house by the path through the gardens and sat for a while on a white marble seat surrounded by a hedge full of large red flowers. Deep in thought, she failed to hear footsteps pass on the far side of the hedge and so was shaken when a deep voice intruded into her thoughts a few minutes later.

'No need to jump to your feet. I wondered what had happened to you. We are supposed to be entertaining guests in ten minutes and Connie said you weren't to be found.'

'I'm sorry, I forgot,' she started guiltily.

A frown drew Kane's brows down over his nose as he asked, 'Are you ill?'

'No, just tired.'

Rising to her feet, she made to leave but his hand on her arm restrained her.

'Look, don't bother about tonight. I'll ask Pilar to stand in.'

Anxious as she was for Juan Carlos and Gilbert, she could have burst out laughing at the thought of Pilar in the role of stand-in. sobering thoughts replaced humour when she realised that by allowing Pilar to replace her she was giving the woman a perfect opportunity to tell Kane about the secret lessons.

'Just give me five minutes,' she reassured him with a smile and ran up the verandah steps and into the house.

The lounge was full of people when she came back downstairs. Kane was nowhere to be seen. Connie was admitting the last of the guests as Frances returned to the hall.

'Have you seen Kane?' she asked Connie.

'Si, he and Gilbert are in the office.'

48

Frances's heart nearly left her body. So, Gilbert had decided to face the rage of the tiger himself rather than let Pilar twist the facts, which she surely would do.

Moving back into the lounge, she began to circulate, making excuses for Kane's absence, answering questions as best she could and fending off those she could not.

When Kane did arrive, he found everything running smoothly and Frances amidst a group of laughing women. Their eyes met across the room and Frances immediately made her apologies, left the group and made her way across the floor to join him.

'Thank you,' he said in a voice like dried ice.

The evening was a great success. When the last guest had departed, Kane came back into the house as Frances was about to climb the stairs to her room. He crossed the floor to where she stood on the third step, so they were eye to eye when he spoke.

'I meant what I said earlier. Thank you for holding everything together for me.

He looked strained and tired and for a moment she almost felt sorry for him. She wanted very much to ask him what had happened between himself and Gilbert, but she bit her tongue and only said softly, 'You're welcome.'

Then she turned and continued up the stairs.

CHAPTER FIVE

Kane was off to Belgium for the next two weeks and Gilbert had said K nothing of what had passed between them the evening of the dinner party. Everything was as it had always been except that Juan Carlos no longer came for his lessons, and no-one had seen sight of or heard a word about Pilar.

Frances was wandering through one of the barns of stabling instead of going back to the office after the siesta when the horse pushed his head over the door of the box in front of her.

'Hello,' she said, putting a hand out to rub his nose.

About to pass on, she stopped and, opening the stable door, moved into the box.

'Firefly, it is you,' she whispered. 'But I don't understand. What are you doing here?'

She stroked his silky neck. There was no doubt in her mind that this was the same horse who had shown such racing potential, now owned by Senora Mendoza who wanted Kane to train him up as an event horse.

She shook her head. There was something very wrong here. Pilar must have paid a fortune for him, as a racer, so why try to change him into something he wasn't?

It was here Gilbert found her.

'I see for myself your love of the horse. Soon we will have you riding again, no? But not this one, I think.'

Frances frowned. She hated having lied to this friendly man but she also hated the sympathy that automatically followed any time she explained why she could not ride for the present and the probing questions her answers prompted.

She stroked the soft muzzle that pushed at her hand. Worst of all was the thought of Kane finding out she had lied. Following the accident which had left her with broken facial bones, collar bone and two broken arms, physiotherapy had done wonders and given her back her independence, but nothing could prevent the pain that still haunted her. That pain had improved in Tenerife's sunny climate but was still a constant reminder of what she had suffered.

Yet she missed the feel of a horse beneath her and the wind in her hair. It was tempting to ignore all the advice and agree to Gilbert's offer of lessons. He thought her shy of horses since a childhood fall so would not put her on anything too strong.

She played with the idea until evening when she told Gilbert she would give it a try. He was delighted. Later, while drinking their coffee, Gilbert told her that he was still teaching Juan Carlos.

'The boy's potential is too great to be

ignored. This I tell to the senor who would not deliberately deny any person a right to advancement. Unhappily, he does not want to know of the boy's existence but has allowed us the use of a small herders' hut in the mountains.'

'May I come with you when you go?' Frances asked eagerly.

Gilbert laid down his empty coffee cup and made to rise.

'It is a little way from here, Fran. I have to go in my own time and by my own transport. The road is rough and would soon damage a vehicle, so I ride. Perhaps when I see how your riding improves I will take you. Now, I must say good-night.'

Frances remained on the verandah calling herself all the names of stupidity she could think of. If she had been honest with him she could have ridden over there on his next visit. Now all she could hope for was to impress him with her riding skills so he would take her with him sooner rather than later.

The evening of Kane's return from Belgium was a shock to Frances. He looked so tried and drawn. Angrily, he made no effort to socialise, merely calling in to let them know he was back then leaving almost immediately for his house on the other side of the ranch.

Frances, who had been storing up grievances against him on behalf of Gilbert and Juan Carlos, found herself comforting a worried Connie.

'We should send a doctor to him. He his ill, I know this. He works too long.'

'He'll be all right after a rest, you'll see,' Frances comforted, but the little woman would not be assured.

'I have known him always, since he was a little boy when his mother ran off and left him with the old senor. He was a wicked old man, the old senor,' she said, shaking her fist at an invisible foe. 'The boy grew wild. Too much freedom is not good. When the Grandfather died, the mother of the senor returned with a husband. The husband had a daughter a few years younger than the boy.'

Connie nodded her head, where she sat opposite Frances at the kitchen table, a faraway look in her eyes.

'Oh, she was trouble, that one,' she spat out as though to rid herself of a nasty taste.

Later, in her room, Frances thought over the old woman's story and tried to visualise the young Kane. She had known what it was like to grow up with an elderly grandparent but whereas her life had been very restricted his had been the opposite. She wondered what it would have been like and how she would have felt if her mother had come home and brought a new husband.

Why had Connie hated the girl? What had she done that happy-go-lucky Connie could not forgive after all this time? The questions were still going in her head as she fell asleep.

*   *   *

The following morning, when Pru arrived in her office with a list of tack repairs needing to go to the saddler, Frances asked her if she knew anything of Kane's family.

'No, not really, why?'

'I was just curious to know who lived with him in that house on the other side of the ranch.'

Pru laughed.

'Thinking of moving in with him?'

'Not on your life. I heard his mother was still alive, that's all.'

'He lives alone, that I do know.'

Pru was leaning against the doorpost and shot forward when an angry voice asked Frances if there was anything else he could furnish her with. 'Far more reliable from the horse's mouth, as they say.'

Pru disappeared out of the door and Frances could feel the heat rise into her face.

'I'm sorry,' she said, refusing to meet his eyes. 'Connie was worried about you last night and I was trying to ascertain if there was anyone at your home to look after you.'

'Connie worries too much,' he said dismissively.

There was a deep silence for a time that jarred Frances's nerves and made her stop

54

what she was doing.

'Well,' she said, raising her head and looking directly across the room at him, 'you did look dreadful last night.'

'And do I look any better today?'

She was caught in his stare and another wave of heat burst forth.

'You improve with a shave,' she caught herself saying, then, shocked at her own temerity, she looked away.

He was laughing, a soft chuckling laugh, laughing at her embarrassment, she seethed.

CHAPTER SIX

Well, it was certainly different, Frances thought as she followed Gilbert into a small paddock. She was sitting straight up in the centre of the horse's back as she had done when a child at the riding school.

After spending several years as an adult perched upon a slip of a saddle with knees hunched up on the animals withers, her present position felt strange indeed. Unable to hide the secret smile as she wondered what Martin would say could he see her now, she shortened the reins and urged the horse into a trot.

Half an hour later, Gilbert was not a happy man. She hung her head as he came over to stand by her horse.

'You are not afraid of this horse, senorita.'

She shook her head.

'You have been riding for a long time, if somewhat badly.' His frown wrinkled his face. 'You waste my time,' he added and stamped off across the paddock.

Frances followed him back to the stable and handed the horse over to the groom. Gilbert was in the tack room flicking through some feed bills when she caught up with him.

'Gilbert, I'm sorry I let you think I was afraid of riding but there were reasons why I didn't want anyone to know that I could ride.'

He shrugged his shoulders and continued to read.

'It wasn't all a lie. I did have an accident but it wasn't years ago, it was sixteen months ago and it didn't put me off riding, but it did mean that I was told I shouldn't ride for the present.'

He swung round then, his eyes full of concern.

'Why did you not tell us this?'

Frances gripped the edges of the table she was leaning against, her natural reluctance to talking about herself weighing heavily on her mind.

'I wanted to keep it simple. I'm here as a secretary until my arms are strong enough to hold the reins again. I thought if people knew I could ride they would want to know why I didn't.'

Gilbert was frowning again.

'I do not understand. You ride with the knees. The hands must only be gentle to guide the horse.'

'I'm a race jockey, Gilbert.'

The shock and amazement on his face would have been funny in different circumstances.

'Ah, now I understand why you ride so badly. I have a lesson now but we will meet this evening and you will tell me all, si?'

For the rest of the day, her arms ached

intolerably, not because of anything she had done to aggravate them, more, she suspected, because of her tense state of mind. She was not given to confidences and sharing, not even to the Truscotts, so to open her heart to Gilbert would be a break from her normal pattern of behaviour.

By late evening, when she was due to meet Gilbert, she was a whirlpool of emotions.

'I thought we would have more privacy at my home,' he told her as he escorted her to the Jeep.

They drove away from the ranch and out on to a narrow, dusty road, until they came to a row of cottages by the roadside. Leaving the car tucked into a gap beneath the house Gilbert led her up the path and into his home. A pretty woman greeted them in her own language then left them with a wave.

'She goes to the house of our neighbour,' Gilbert explained after introducing his wife, 'to gossip, you understand.'

When they were both comfortable and Gilbert had poured the wine, they sat in silence as Frances decided how much she would tell of her past. In the end she told him everything. He let her talk without interruption and then there was silence again.

'Thank you,' he said in acknowledgement of her confidence.

'My arms may never be strong enough to race again but I will ride and would love to come with you to see Juan Carlos.

'You will ride for me each day and soon we will see the boy together.' Gilbert was as good as his word and made time to watch her ride most days. Kane also noticed and mentioned it in passing one day in the office. 'How do you feel up on a horse again?'

'Fine, thank you,' she said but kept her eyes on her work.

He was standing with his back to her, studying the calendar on the wall behind her.

'I'll be going away shortly to Munich for two days. I would like you to accompany me. I'll be lecturing and will need someone to take notes and organise my time there.'

Frances thought she was going to choke. She snapped the top on her pen and fiddled with the papers in front of her.

'What about my work here?'

'It will only be for two days. You will catch up easily when we return.'

He had returned to the front of the desk as he spoke and was looking down at her.

'You have done a good job helping me socialise with the horsemasters, now you must widen the experience.'

This I can do without, Frances fretted. Supposing I bump into someone from the racing fraternity who recognises me? How do I explain that away? She was still worrying about the situation long after Kane had left.

'What am I going to do?' she begged

Gilbert later that evening when they were sitting alone on the verandah with their coffee.

Gilbert ran his fingers through his hair.

'Tell the truth. A little misleading is not a sin.'

Frances was shaking her head.

'No, it might be a little misleading to you, Gilbert, but believe me, it will be a sin to him.'

Gilbert laughed.

'You have been here only a short time, but you know already.' Frances felt the blood run to her face.

'Well, no, not really, but, well, he didn't want me here in the first place. I've worked hard and he's accepted me. If he finds out I've lied to him he might just fire me after all.'

'No, senorita, you are his secretary, not his pupil. He will have no interest in your reasons for coming here, only your ability to do your job.' But Frances was not convinced.

*　　　*　　　*

The day of the visit to Munich dawned bright and sunny. Frances had packed a few essentials into a straw bag she had bought at the local market and dressed in the smart lightweight suit she had arrived in.

Kane made no comment as they climbed into the station wagon and headed off to the airport. On their arrival at the ticket desk, the bottom fell out of Frances's stomach when they were joined by Pilar Mendoza. She came forward and kissed Kane on both cheeks before casting a disdainful glance at Frances. Ignoring Kane's introduction, she clung to his arm and talked incessantly until they were aboard the plane and settled into their seats.

They travelled first class which delighted Frances who sat alone across the aisle from Kane and Pilar. They had to change planes on mainland Spain and here, much to Frances's relief, Pilar left them.

After arriving in Germany in the middle of the afternoon, they discovered that the suite Frances had booked at their hotel had one double bedroom instead of two.

To say the look she received from Kane was suspicious was an understatement. He looked absolutely furious as he strutted impatiently back and forth in front of the reception desk. However, soon everything was cleared up and they were settling in.

'If you're ready I would like you to accompany me to my first meeting, in five minutes.'

The tone was brisk, the face as impassive as ever but the eyes were saying something else as she turned to regard him, standing just inside her bedroom door.

'We'll go straight on to dinner after the meeting,' he said, then turned back into the lounge.

The meeting went well and soon they were on their way back to the hotel dining-room. They were halfway through their dessert when the entrance to the dining-room was filled with a party of chattering people. A swirl of dark green stopped by their table and Frances knew without looking up that Pilar had found them again. With a red carnation in her dark hair and diamonds on her wrist and finger she looked dangerously beautiful.

She was introducing her friends to Kane while Frances sat quietly by until a familiar name broke through her thoughts. She listened carefully to what was being said about Firefly.

After a hectic two days, they returned to Tenerife. Frances was welcomed back by everyone as though they had never expected to see her again, all, that was, except Maurice.

'He's gone over to the Mendoza ranch and taken that horse of hers with him,' Pru told her.

'Firefly?'

Pru nodded.

'Maurice says he isn't coming back, that the Mendoza woman has offered him a job. Kane will be furious when he has to find another instructor at such short notice.'

'Why take Firefly?' Frances was puzzled. 'I thought Kane was schooling him.'

'Perhaps they've fallen out,' Pru said with a shrug.

'Well, there was no sign of it when she was with us on our flight out or when she bumped into us in the hotel.'

'She was in Germany, too?' Pru asked, startled. 'I don't understand. If she was abroad, how come Maurice told us she had invited him over and persuaded him to take on the overall management of the place?'

'He has also placed the training of the horse into the hands of Paul Drago,' Eduardo said.

'Oh, no.' The others looked up at Frances's cry of distress. 'Kane said this Drago would ruin Firefly.'

'You've become very attached to that horse, haven't you?' Pru said, reaching forward to pat her on the arm.

Eduardo leaned forward and said, 'Kane takes time with the horse, plays with him, persuades him that he wants to do as Kane asks. Drago is good trainer, too, but he demands obedience. The animal must learn,' and he clicked his fingers, 'quickly.'

'Firefly is young and not bred to be an event horse. Anyone can see that. I'm surprised Kane didn't,' Frances went on.

'Oh, I think he did, Fran, but for his own reasons he keeps Senora Mendoza happy.'

'Why? What does she have apart from the obvious, to persuade him to do a thing like that, to deliberately spoil a good horse?'

She was angry and worried about the horse

and what would happen to him.

'Walk with me,' Gilbert said. offering his hand to her.

She was about to decline, saying she was tired, but one look into his face made her rise to her feet and accompany him down the steps of the verandah and across the grass to the gardens. He didn't waste any time. 'Senora Mendoza owns the hillside on the far side of the valley.'

'Where you rest the school horses?'

'Si. It has been leased for many generations and soon that lease must be renewed. It is thought the senora might not agree to this. It will break with tradition to do this but . . .'

He shrugged expressively.

'And without the land?' Frances dared to ask.

Gilbert hung his head on one side.

'It would be difficult. Good grazing is hard to find. Most of the northern valleys are given over to agriculture.'

They talked for a little longer then Frances excused herself for being tired and went to her room. She sat out on the balcony in her nightdress and listened to the whispering trees and the clicking song of the crickets.

CHAPTER SEVEN

A letter came the very next day to tell Frances that her friend, Tessa, had given birth to a baby boy, weighing eight-and-a-half pounds. Both mother and baby were fine. Martin had kicked up a fuss when Tessa had returned home only two days after the birth but the baby was good and Tessa glad to be home.

Tears rolled down Frances's cheeks as she read it. How she would have loved to be there. Why didn't she just pack up and go back? Her arms were getting stronger every day and even if she couldn't ride, there were other jobs she could do back in England.

She put the letter back in its envelope and dropped it to her lap. Self pity, this was. How her grandmother would have scoffed. Somehow horses weren't enough any more. She longed for a little of what her friends Martin and Tessa shared.

Shocked by her feelings, she put the letter in her pocket and went through to the office. There, she found Maurice's letter of resignation lying on her desk. Her fingers itched to open it but she left it for Kane. He stormed into the office an hour later, snatched up Maurice's letter and left without a word.

Frances went for an early lunch and returned to the office at half-past one when she would normally have been resting. Some work needed finishing off and she wanted to be away early that afternoon to go with Gilbert to see Juan Carlos.

She crossed the patio, her soft sandals making little noise. At first she saw no-one beyond the shadow of the doorway. Then as she passed from the bright sunlight into the interior of the office, she saw Kane sitting slumped in the chair in front of her desk.

Only the movement of the tree tops and the tinkle of the fountain broke the silence. She wondered if he was sleeping, he was so still. Standing silently behind him, she watched him.

'How long are you going to stand there watching me?'

Frances jumped and leaped forward like a startled deer.

'I'm sorry! Can I help with something?'

She made her way around the desk and sat down.

'No. What are you doing here? It's far too hot to work.'

'I came to finish some work I started this morning. I want to get away early this afternoon.'

'Why?'

Her hand stilled above the keyboard.

'Why what?'

'Why do you want to get away early?'

'It will be my own time.'

'I'm not disputing the fact. I'm simply enquiring what you are doing later.'

He made it sound so normal a request, what was she to say? That she was going to watch the progress of the young man he had forbidden from the ranch.

'Riding lessons,' she said and held her breath.

'Then I shall come and watch you.'

He smiled as Frances felt her heart cease to function.

'Please, don't. It will only upset my concentration.'

He laughed, and said, 'I wish more people would say that instead of demanding so much of my time.'

Thinking it wise to change the subject, Frances asked him about Firefly. A change came over his features as he pushed himself up in the chair and made to rise.

'I have taken him off the livery list but wondered about training fees,' she added, head bent forward over her keyboard.

After a moment, she heard him slump back into the chair again and risked a glance up through her lashes. A dark frown lowered over his eyes as his fingers played an impatient tattoo on the arm of the chair.

'You can take Beckworth off the payroll, too.'

'I already have.'

It must have been something in her voice

for he glanced across at her from his chair and his features lightened.

'It's a pity about the horse but he really wasn't suitable. So, yes, you can strike the training fees.'

'What's going to happen to him?' she asked anxiously.

'To Beckworth or the horse?'

She gave an impatient shake of her head.

'Firefly, of course.'

'Gilbert said you were attached to him. I'd like to say he has a good future ahead of him, but that wouldn't be true. Oh, he might make the grade initially but I doubt he will last long. Pilar will probably tire of him and sell him on.'

'What on earth made her buy a racer in the first place?'

'What makes you think he was a racer?'

The sharp question brought her up with a start.

'Oh, his movements and the fact that he is a thoroughbred.'

Her insides sighed with relief as he appeared to accept her reasoning. 'It's always thoroughbreds,' he said, half to himself. 'Pilar likes to look good in the ring and she does at the dressage and show jumping.

Unfortunately the cross country takes stamina, not looks.'

'Why has she done this?'

'Put Beckworth in charge of the Ranch Faro, you mean?' He shrugged. 'I wasn't even aware that she knew him all that well.'

'Is she back from Germany?'

'Yes.'

'If you told her the horse was no good, would she believe you?'

His eyebrows rose as he glanced across at her from where he sat stretched out in the chair.

'I already did and yes, she believed me.'

'Then I don't understand why he is with this Drago person.'

'That will be Beckworth's doing.'

Frances bit down hard on her lip, trying not to let him see how agitated she was. Kane rose from his seat and, crossing to the desk, placed two hands on the top and leaned forward, his face close to her own.

'You really are attached to this animal, aren't you? I'll see what I can find out.

With that, he turned from the desk and left the office.

* * *

Frances was smiling when she met Gilbert later that afternoon. He had led out the quiet little mare, Sophia, for Frances. She put her foot into the stirrup and swung up into the saddle.

'I am pleased to see you looking happier today.' Gilbert grinned.

'Why not? I'm looking forward to an

69

exciting outing and Kane has promised to find out what is to happen to Firefly.'

Frances laughed out loud as Gilbert's ears seemed to rise with his eyebrows at her news.

They rode out of the yard and down on to the road. The place Gilbert brought her to was not as comfortable as the large school on the ranch but only a fenced ring with a small hut to one side in front of which was a bench. They tied their horses to the fence and Frances crossed to the bench and sat down.

In broad, brimmed hat, dark glasses, jodhpurs and shirt, she emptied a bag of extras she had brought with her. There was water, fruit and chocolate, in case anyone was hungry or thirsty. Juan Carlos now rode a tall bay horse that Frances had never seen before. It wasn't quite as supple as the grey stallion and it took all of the boy's skill to get the best out of the animal.

They still looked good, however, and Frances clapped enthusiastically when the session was over. The horse was tied to the rail with the others and the two men drank gratefully from the flask of water that Frances offered them.

They chatted amiably for an hour before Gilbert said it was time to leave. As she and Gilbert rode back over the rough hillside and down into the valley, Frances asked him what he thought her chances were of rescuing

Firefly.

'I would have to be able to buy him then fly him home. My friends, the Truscotts, would take him in and care for him. If Kane can persuade her to sell him to me then with Martin's know-how I'm sure we can manage the paper work and formalities.'

Racing on in her enthusiasm, she failed to notice Gilbert's silence.

Once back at the stables, Gilbert placed an arm around her shoulders and led her up through the gardens.

'It is extremely unlikely that the senora will release this horse.'

'But if Kane . . .'

'Because Kane will not ask it of her. He will ask after the animal's welfare, si, but he cannot pressure her to part with it and if he did it would only encourage her to withhold it.'

'But surely, the horse is no good to her.'

'She is a difficult woman. She has caused much trouble in the past for many people. If Kane says she is to sell the horse then I will know someone who will attempt to buy him for you. This way it will not come back to the senor and the ranch. Agreed?'

'Agreed.'

Pilar was at dinner with the horsemasters that evening and determined to play hostess in place of Frances.

'What a jealous cat,' Pru remarked as

71

Frances sat down beside her after giving up all pretence of partnering Kane in mixing with the clients during the pre-dinner drinks.

'A dangerous cat,' Frances replied. 'Robert Shand particularly wanted to talk to me about extending his stay, but madam cut in and bedazzled the poor lad and led him off before he knew what was happening.'

'Well, she's welcome to Maurice. They deserve each other, those two.'

'Oh, you mean his new job? Yes, that was a hasty piece of undercover work.'

Pru chuckled.

'I suppose you could call it undercover, but under the covers would be more like it.'

Frances stared.

'What are you saying, Pru? Pilar is here, hanging on to Kane's arm as though she owned it. He wouldn't have her in the house if that was the case.

'Who's going to tell him?'

Frances opened her mouth, then shut it, swallowing hard when she realised the significance of Pru's statement.

'You?' Pru asked.

Frances thought of how easy he had been to talk to in the office, then shook her head.

'No, I wouldn't want to have to.'

'Exactly.' Pru nodded.

Frances thought deeply all evening. Alone in her room that night, she began to put her thoughts together. By the time she fell asleep, she knew what she had to do.

*   *   *

'So you see, an affair with Maurice would gain her nothing,' she told Gilbert the next morning. 'It could be construed as a small strike against Kane as could the loss of the valley grazing. The horse is of no concern to him at all. So what is she trying to prove?'

Gilbert's face was grim when eventually she stopped talking.

'What is it? What do you think she is planning?' Frances persisted. 'It is as it was before.'

'What is?'

'It is a long story, Frances. Meet me in the tack room after the mid-day feed and I will tell you of it. If what you say about Senora Mendoza and Maurice is true, then there will be trouble for the senor and we must find some way to stop it.'

When she arrived back at the office, Pilar Mendoza was sitting on the corner of the desk, flicking through some files.

'What are you doing in here?'

Frances's voice was as stiff and cold as she could make it.

Pilar made a small pout with her lips and replaced the files on the desk. 'When Kane and I marry, you will be the first to go.'

She slid to her feet and walked out leaving

73

a dumbstruck Frances.

It wasn't possible surely! Kane would never marry her just to hang on to his grazing. Of course he wouldn't, she scolded herself. The woman is just indulging in wishful thinking. All the same, she decided Gilbert must be told. The morning flashed by and soon it was time to meet Gilbert in the tack room. He was sitting on a high stool by the table, his foot swinging idly to and fro, obviously deep in thought, as though what he was about to tell her was bothering him. She sat on a small stool and waited.

'Many years ago, when Kane's mother returned after the death of her father, she brought with her a husband and his daughter. The girl was flighty and attracted to Kane. When she became pregnant, Kane was blamed. He denied responsibility, saying the baby wasn't his. There was a lot of bad talk stirred up against the girl and not long after the child was born, the girl died in an accident. Kane was sent away and his mother and stepfather later went to live in Australia. The child was brought up by his true parent. That is the story that is told.'

Frances waited.

'And?'

Gilbert shrugged.

'It was no secret at the time that Pilar wanted Kane for herself. Her husband died two years ago.'

'So now her husband is dead, she is after him again. So why get involved with Maurice?'

She told Gilbert what had happened in the office.

'Do you think she really is engaged to Kane or is it just wishful thinking?'

'I think Kane is not so much a fool, but she is a scheming woman. Who knows what she is up to? We must be on our guard.'

'If he were to turn her down again, would you say she was a danger to him?'

Gilbert cocked his head on one side and spoke in a gentle voice.

'You care for him, I think. To answer your questions, yes, I believe you are both in danger.'

Frances took a step back.

'I dislike Pilar very much and am anxious for Firefly, that's all.'

'Of course,' Gilbert said and nodded gravely.

On the point of finishing for the day, she looked up to find Kane watching her from the doorway. He came into the room, sat down at his desk and asked her to take a letter.

Normally he would simply leave it on the machine and she could copy it off the following morning.

It was a letter to a solicitor, confirming an agreement to a deal made between three parties, one of whom resided in Germany and one in France. This was going to enhance all parties' shares provided it didn't come to the public's notice. The parties were named and she recognised a world-famous German company of saddlers.

'I want it sent first thing in the morning. I can trust your discretion, I hope,' Kane said.

Frances was outraged but before she could give way to her indignation, Kane turned, moved over to her desk and placed a small parcel in front of her.

'I bought this in Germany, a small thank-you for all your hard work since joining us here. With all the business that has happened since, I forgot about it.'

He left a shocked Frances staring at the small parcel as though it might run away if she moved. Later in her room, after her shower, she unwrapped the present. To her delight, it was a china horse on the point of leaping into a discipline taught in The Spanish Riding School of Vienna.

She gazed at it a long time, smoothing its delicate body between her fingers as she now recalled watching him going into the shop in Munich and how long she had waited for him to come out, then given up. She swallowed the lump in her throat then placed the precious item back in its wrappings and tucked it into a drawer.

CHAPTER EIGHT

Kane was as good as his word and came back to Frances with the information that Firefly was doing well and Pilar intended entering him in the Birmington horse trials in England in two months time. Frances was devastated.

'Will you be entering?'

'Of course, and I shall want you with me.'

She stood and stared at him, bereft of words. She could only gulp air like a fish out of water. When at last she managed to formulate some words they were, 'No, no, I can't.'

A deep frown creased his brow and his eyes narrowed as though to ward off strong light.

'Why would you not want to visit your friends?'

She could hear suspicion in his voice. Her thoughts flew this way and that, searching for a way out of her dilemma. There was no reason to believe that the Truscotts would be at the horse trials, but it was a certainty that someone from the racing fratern,ty would be there, then her secret would be all out in the open.

Would it really bother him to hear that his secretary was actually a has-been jockey, she wondered. Perhaps Giiert was right and it wasn't a secret worth trying to keep. So she gave him the best smile she could muster.

'I'd love to go, but it's one of the busiest times on the ranch. We're booked solid.'

She didn't like the look in his eyes as he gave her a brief nod of the head. 'It'll be seen to,' he said with a twist to his mouth.

In the office, a fax came through that had to be sorted then she worked on the payroll after which she watered her flowers, but all the time her mind was on the horse trials in ten weeks. Did Kane really believe that Firefly would be ready in time? If Pilar was planning to harm Kane or Firefly in some way, would this be the occasion? Perhaps an unforeseen accident or some dreadful damage to the ranch's reputation. It never for an instant occurred to her that perhaps her own safety was in question.

Gilbert's reply to her worries, when she met up with him at lunch, was simple.

'No, it is not possible, even with a clever, willing horse, to train him to that standard in the length of time she has owned him. If he had not been so green perhaps, but as it is, no.'

Frances sighed.

'Then why is she going?'

'The Senora Mendoza does not take rejection lightly. If the marriage she brags about does not happen, then she will take revenge. Neither Kane nor your horse will be safe.'

78

She shook her head.

'He wants me to go with him.'

'He knows the horse is of great importance to you, that you would wish to watch his performance.'

She rose from her seat and, moving over to the verandah rail, looked out over the green paddocks and dry, dusty tracks. Hedges alive with flowers led down through the gardens to the barns and schools below. Gilbert moved up behind her.

'You will be in the best place to watch over both Kane and the horse and to see that no harm comes to either.'

She stiffened, then turned to look at him, her eyes questioning. He gave a little nod and then moved away.

* * *

The flight back to England took them just over four hours. There was no sign of Pilar on the plane for which Frances was immensely grateful. Over the past several weeks she had been a real thorn in Frances's side, constantly at the ranch and on three separate occasions she'd been in the office while Frances was out, making Frances lock the door every time she left.

When she was riding, Pilar would be hanging over the fence with a running commentary to Gilbert, who ignored her.

Frances tried not to let this behaviour upset her and went out of her way to avoid the woman, but she 48 was everywhere or so it seemed. Even in her dreams, she would wake in a sweat as Firefly and Kane sat writhing on the ground beneath a broken fence. Of course it was all a load of rubbish for Kane didn't even ride Firefly.

She dismissed her fears as they prepared to leave the plane on landing. Outside the airport, a car waited to take them to their hotel then on to the trial grounds. Kane's horse, Commander, would already be there in his makeshift stable with his groom.

The rap on the door of her hotel bedroom made her jump even though she was expecting it. Opening the door she was ready, but scowled crossly as Maurice Beckworth pushed into the room.

'What are you doing here?'

'I've come to keep you company. Thought we could do the town together.'

'What on earth are you talking about, you creep! Get out. I'm expecting Kane any minute.'

He was smiling, a sly smile.

'I don't think so,' he said. 'He's dining privately with a friend. You and I can do the town and I'll even buy you a slap-up meal. What do you say?'

But he wasn't waiting for her answer, instead he was holding out the jacket she had lain over the back of the chair. These tactics had been used many times before on Frances as the rare female in racing circles. She had learned early to stand her ground. Now she took the jacket out of his hands and placed it back on the chair. Then she picked up the phone and dialled Kane's room number.

Maurice made a dive to stop her but she swung away from him. The phone was ringing at the other end but no-one was picking it up. Frowning, she replaced the receiver.

'Now do you believe me?' Maurice grunted, rubbing his ribs where she had dug him with her elbow.

'Whether he's there or not I have no intention of going out with you. Now please leave before I call security.'

'But I was . . .'

'Out.'

She opened the door wide and stood to one side. He hesitated, rocking from one foot to the other, grumbling to himself, then with a huffy growl, he left.

Two minutes later, Kane knocked on her door.

'Was that Beckworth I saw leaving?'

'He tried to get me to go out with him. He said you would be occupied elsewhere.'

'What is he doing here?'

'I haven't the faintcst idea.'

Picking up her jacket, she joined him in the doorway. They made their 49 way together along the corridor and into the elevator. On the ground floor they were crossing the foyer when Pilar accosted them. Frances moved a discreet distance away and watched Pilar working her magic. Kane looked over Pilar's head and his glance connected with Frances, but she turned away, breaking eye contact, and praying that he fell in with Pilar's demands and didn't upset her at this point.

He indicated she join them and all three made there way out to the car waiting to take them to Birmington Park. Once there, they checked on Commander and his groom to make sure all was well. The horse nibbled Kane's pockets until he was given the expected titbit. Frances noted the closeness of the two and understood how the horse would give his best for this man.

Pilar stayed outside talking to the groom. Farther down the row, Firefly's head appeared over the half door. As they walked towards him, he shied back into the rear of the box.

This upset Frances more than she could say. It was obvious to her that the animal was nervous and unhappy. She hurried ahead of the other two and spoke gently over the stable door. He eyed her nervously then gradually relaxed and eased forward to stretch his nose out towards her.

A hand fell on to her shoulder and she looked up into Kane's face. Pilar spoke from behind.

'Drago has done wonders with him. I really think I stand a good chance this year. What do you think, Kane? Isn't he in great shape?'

She pushed through between them to open the door and pat the horse's neck.

'He's in good condition, Pilar,' Kane agreed.

'He's a beauty, aren't you, boy?' she said with pride.

That evening, they dined together in the hotel but there was no mention of Beckworth. Afterwards Pilar thanked Kane gracefully for the meal and departed to her own hotel.

I wonder why she doesn't stay here, Frances wondered, as many of the other competitors appear to be doing so.

'It's early yet. Would you like a drink?'

Kane indicated the bar. Soft music played in the background and apart from two or three couples sitting around small tables, the bar was empty. Before she had made her mind up one way or the other, she found herself being led forward and seated at the bar.

'What would you like?' he inquired.

'Tonic and pineapple, please.'

He gave her a quizzical look before ordering her drink and a brandy for himself.

'I don't drink alcohol,' she said, angry with herself for feeling that she owed him an explanation.

They fell into a discussion about horses and Frances was carried away in her enthusiasm of the subject and failed to realise her mistake until she caught herself mentioning a famous name in racing. With a warm feeling flooding her cheeks, she dropped her eyes to her glass. When she raised her chin cautiously and glanced across the table, Kane was leaning forward, his hands cupping the brandy glass.

'You were saying,' he said, showing an innocent interest.

'He's a friend of the Truscotts.'

'Ah. What exactly does Martin Truscott do for a living? He gave you a glowing reference but failed to mention what kind of business he was in.'

'He's a vet.'

'Well, I suppose that explains why you are so knowledgeable about horses. A large animal vet, is he?'

'Yes, horses and farm animals.'

Finishing her drink in quick, nervous sips, she shook her head when he asked if she wanted another.

'No, thank you. I'll go up now. Good-night.'

'Don't be in such a hurry,' he said as she made to rise. 'I'll walk up with you.'

At her door, he said, 'Sleep well, Fran, if you feel you would like to skip the trials for an afternoon to see your friends please do so.'

Once in her room, she stood with her back to the door, her heart making odd jumps. It was the first time he had called her Fran and it made her feel shaky, anxious. She wasn't quite sure why, but one thing she did know was she had never felt like it before.

The next morning, she made her own way to the park after a late breakfast. The following three days were to be like a holiday with little expected of her except to be on hand if needed. However, threatening danger demanded that she stayed close to both Kane and Firefly.

Both horses were in the practice ring awaiting their turn at the dressage. Kane brought Commander up to where she stood at the rope. Tony, the groom, stood nearby with brush and sponge handy in case a hair might be blown out of place or a spot of dirt mar the polished hooves. Kane looked magnificent in tall hat and cravat, his boots like mirrors reflecting the glint of spurs on his heels. The steel work on the horses tack had been polished within an inch of its existence. The whole turnout made Frances's heart swell with pride.

She felt the hint of a silly grin across her mouth and was aware of the curious glances of onlookers as Kane bent forward from the saddle to ask her to meet him for lunch.

'Oh, I brought it with me actually. I thought it might be easier here in case you were busy,' she replied.

'Very astute,' he said, a grin taking the harshness from the words. 'May 51 one ask where you left this promising meal?'

'In the stable.'

Kane spoke to the groom in Spanish. Tony came forward and placed his gear on the ground by Frances's feet then ran off.

'He's gone to fetch lunch. He'll take it to wherever you want it. In the meantime, look after his kit.'

He raised a hand and trotted off as his name was called. Frances was unaware of anyone standing next to her until Maurice spoke.

'You can run after Harding as much as you want, it's no skin off my nose, but she won't take kindly to it.'

He nodded to where Pilar, sitting astride a restless-looking Firefly, was talking to a slim man of medium height in a dark suit.

Trying to keep track of what the speaker was announcing about Kane's performance, while being pestered by Maurice, drove her to snap at him. He took immediate umbrage and stalked away just as Tony returned with the picnic hamper.

When Kane came back into the practice area, Pilar was the first to move forward to congratulate him. As she did so, the man she had been talking to crossed to the entrance of the ring and made his way over to the area set aside for the horseboxes. Frances couldn't be sure but she thought she saw him meet up with Maurice and together they climbed into the cab of one of the boxes.

Tony picked up the hamper and his kit and

they headed up a grassy hill, around to a point where they could watch the rest of the horses being put through their paces. Once Frances was settled, Tony set off again to see Commander.

Someone was blocking her line of vision and it was Pilar's turn in the ring. She sat and seethed for several minutes then decided to push forward herself. Firefly was behaving beautifully and Pilar really did look good. As they passed by, however, Frances noticed the horse was sweating and wide-eyed. When they had finished and left the ring, the animal ducked and dived around the throng of people to follow their movements.

'Not a happy horse, wouldn't you say?'

Much to her annoyance, she swung around to face Maurice again.

'Ah, ha,' he said as Frances opened her mouth to give him a tongue lashing. 'I come in peace, bearing gifts.'

'I don't want your silly gifts.'

She ground her teeth and made to walk away. Keeping pace with her, he grabbed her arm and pulled it through his own as though they were the best of friends then he shoved a flat parcel at her.

'Take it,' he said. 'You want the horse, don't you?'

Dropping her arm, he disappeared quickly into the crowd. When she looked up, Kane was walking towards her.

CHAPTER NINE

'I've seen more of Beckworth in the last two days than I saw of him the entire time he worked for me,' Kane said as he came alongside her. 'I don't know what he's up to,' Frances remarked, 'but he's a real pest. Shall we eat?'

'This looks very nice,' he said. 'Where did it come from?'

Lowering himself on to the blanket, he eyed the open basket from which Frances was arranging plates and glasses. There were two bottles of wine, one red, one white, smoked salmon on a bed of cream cheese and spinach, Parma ham with little melon balls, chicken legs and a bowl of prepared salad. There were also fresh fruit and mint sweets, all prepared by the hotel chef.

'The hotel,' she said as she kneeled by the basket, a bottle in each hand. 'Red or white?'

'White, I think. What did Beckworth want?'

'Nothing I could make any sense of. He grabbed my arm, pushed me a few yards then stuck a parcel in my hand and left.'

Handing Kane his glass she remembered that Maurice had also hinted that the parcel was something to do with Firefly.

'Was it anything important, the parcel?'

There had been no time to open it. Spilling

the wine she was pouring for herself, she shook her head.

'Will Tony stay with Commander? Shall I save him something to eat?'

'He'll have his own.'

He was watching her closely his eyes never leaving her face.

'Try this,' he said, reaching over the basket that lay between them, and offering her a small parcel of salmon.

Looking up as he spoke, her gaze was momentarily trapped in the brilliance of his eyes. Her mouth opened automatically to receive the food, his fingers touched her lips and a mere instant was frozen in time.

'I haven't had time to look at the parcel yet,' she whispered.

'When do you intend visiting your friends?' he asked, helping himself to chicken and salad.

Frances sipped her wine and thought about their small Yorkshire racing yard.

'It's up North. I don't know that there will be time. I'll phone when I get back to the hotel.'

What with trying to keep an eye out for any danger to Kane or Firefly and longing to see the Truscotts again, Frances felt that she was being pulled every which way. Her anxiety must have shown on her face for after a short pause, Kane broke into her thoughts.

'Why don't I drive you up there on Monday

before we fly back?'

A cloud covered the sun and the breeze brushed goose bumps over her skin. As she was on the point of answering him, there came a growl from the crowd. Kane climbed to his feet to see what had happened in the ring. The incident that was attracting the crowds attention, however, was not in the ring itself but in the practice enclosure.

Frances joined Kane just in time to see a furious Pilar being dragged across the ground by a terrified, retreating Firefly. Kane ran through the crowd to brush aside the two marshals who were flapping their hands and trying to approach the horse. Talking quietly he walked up to Firefly, flung some order to Pilar and gently took hold of the horse's bridle.

The quivering animal had come to a stop as Pilar let go of the reins. Then Kane walked him around to his groom and handed him over with a few words of advice before turning his attention to Pilar, who was shaking herself down. The crowd's interest had returned to the main ring as Kane escorted Pilar to the picnic area.

She was spitting fire in Spanish as Kane thrust a glass of wine into her hand. Swiftly, Frances cleared away the food and repacked the basket. Pilar was insisting upon being taken back to the hotel.

'I must have a word with Tony first, then we

90

will all return to the hotel,' Kane said before he walked off, leaving the two women alone.

Frances didn't like being left in the Spanish woman's company not even for the few minutes it would take Kane to pass on his instructions to the groom, but at least it would give her the opportunity to ask about Firefly.

'How do you think Firefly will stand up to the cross country tomorrow?'

Pilar glared across at her but said nothing. Frances tried again. 'He did well in the ring.'

The woman ignored her, turning to watch Kane's return. He returned a few minutes later minus hat, crop and spurs and led them off to the carpark after taking the picnic basket from Frances's hands.

Back in her room at the hotel, Frances pulled the parcel Maurice had given her out of her pocket. It was in a bulky brown business envelope, wrapped around with sticky tape. Sifting down on the bed, she turned it over in her hands, wondering what she was going to find inside it.

Something to do with saving Firefly, he had said, but she found it hard to believe. What did he care what happened to Firefly? Piece by piece, she tore open the envelope. The sticky tape wouldn't snap and it was tied tightly all around a second parcel inside the envelope.

It took several minutes before the truth dawned. There was nothing here except layers of paper. Frances sat amidst the rubbish scattered over her bed, a deep frown between her brows. What was he up to? Try as she might, she couldn't work out why he had done this.

There was a knock on the door half an hour later and Frances opened it to find Maurice standing in the passage.

'What do you want, and more to the point, what game are you playing pushing bags of rubbish at me?'

She was livid, and made to slam the door in his face, but he shoved a foot in the gap.

'If you really want that horse you'll listen to what I have to say. Now let me in or do you want all and sundry to hear what I have to say?' Reluctantly she stepped aside and allowed him to pass into the room. 'Say what you have to then get out,' she snapped.

He sauntered over to the w!ndow and looked down into the carpark. 'Not much of a view, is it?'

Frances opened her mouth to warn him again when he spoke slowly without turning back into the room.

'Pilar has gone home. She left me the job of selling the horse.'

'She's selling Firefly?'

Frances could hardly believe she had heard right. He swung round, a crafty look on his face.

'No, I am.'

Calm down, she told herself. Don't get carried away. He's up to something.

'Well, you know I want him. Have you come to give me a price?' she began.

'You could say that but why don't *we discuss* that over dinner?'

Oh, no, she groaned to herself. She was supposed to be having dinner with Kane. With his head to one side and a confident grin on his face he watched her indecision.

'Right, fine, I'll have to make a phone call first but I'll meet you downstairs in fifteen minutes,' she replied eventually.

When he'd gone, Frances picked up the phone and stood for several minutes before making a stab at the buttons.

That evening, she phoned the Truscotts. After talking happy baby talk with Tessa for several minutes she asked to speak to Martin. Her friends were thrilled to hear that she was here in England but then she told Martin about Firefly. He remembered the horse and agreed he had shown great potential.

'I want to buy him, Martin.'

There was silence for a while and then Martin asked, 'What's the problem?'

'Money. I want to know if you'd be interested in a share.'

'How much?'

She told him.

'Hang on while I talk to Tess.'

Frances sat on the bed, cradling the phone

93

and chewing her lip.

'OK, how long are you here for?' Martin asked when he spoke again. 'Two more days.'

'You going to be able to make all the arrangements at your end? It is the weekend, you know.'

Breathless with excitement she said, 'I"Il get on to it first thing in the morning.'

'Right, I'll have a banker's daft down to you first thing and a box for the horse. You sure you've thoughf.his out? It's a big responsibility.'

'We'll bring you fame you've bnly dreamed of, you wait and see.' Her voice trembled as she thanked him.

* * *

The following day was the day of the cross country, the day Frances was dreading because if there was going to be any foul play then the cross country was the place for it, even though the rules were carried out with strict precision.

Frances found herself a good spot at the cattle grid with its short, extra stride in the middle that would, if the rider wasn't careful, catch out a long-striding horse like Commander. Kane flew round the course in good time, the agility of the big horse amazing everyone who watched. Frances was on her feet urging them on as they passed through the cattle grid without harm and continued on their way.

Kane was leading the competition at the end of the day leaving only the show jumping to come on the Sunday. So far, so good, Frances told herself when she was alone once more in her room at the hotel. Perhaps it had all been in her imagination and nothing would happen to harm Kane, the ranch or Firefly.

The telephone rang on the bedside table as she came out of the shower. It was Kane asking if she was free in the evening as she owed him for last night's disappointment with the dinner cancellation. She agreed to meet him in twenty minutes and fluttered around wondering what to wear. When at last she decided, and donned the dress, she couldn't decide on the right accessories for it, and so the twenty minutes dwindled away.

When the doorbell rang, she still wasn't ready.

'Please,' she said opening the door wide. 'I'm sorry to keep you but I didn't bring much of a wardrobe.'

'What's wrong? You look fine to me.'

He was smiling, his eyes like soft moss as he looked her over.

'Let me help you into that jacket and we'll take a walk around town and see if we can find ourselves an Italian restaurant. You like Italian food?'

'Yes, I do, as a matter of fact.'

The night air was warm, not as warm as they were used to, of course, which was why she wore a jacket. She had become quite used to the heat of Tenerife and so felt the lack of it though she had only been there six months. They walked side by side, in silence at first.

'How's Commander? Is he still fit?' Feeling a little awkward she hesitated. 'I mean . . .'

'He's fine. There were a couple of obstacles he stumbled over but he recovered splendidly and is sound and ready for tomorrow. I'm afraid we can't say the same for Pilar. Firefly is lame. He finished the course but was found to be lame later. She wasn't very happy about it but she knew there was a risk entering such a green horse.'

Now was the time to tell him she had bought Firefly but hesitated. Fully conscious of the envious glances from women diners following them to their table, Frances realised she was enjoying the reflected glory of her partner. He was quite the most handsome man in the room and well-known to the majority of visitors crowding the town for the famous annual horse trials.

They ate a wonderful pasta, drank lots of red wine and talked about horses, all kinds of horses, but still she couldn't bring herself to mention Firefly.

The next day, Commander jumped two clear rounds but Kane refused to push him and as a result lost out on timing. His overall placing at the end of the trials was second. He shrugged his shoulders, patting the great horse and pulling his ears as he stood in line for the award ceremony. Frances was overwhelmed by a feeling of pride.

It was as though she herself had taken some small part in Kane's success. Perhaps she had for when he had seen Commander safely to his box and checked everything was ready for horse and groom to travel home to Tenerife, he returned to her side and swung her off her feet.

'Tomorrow we will meet with your friends and I will learn all about you.'

'Why?'

Breathlessly she clutched at the lapels of his jacket to steady herself. He set her back at arm's length and studied her face.

'Because we are friends, I think, and I wish to know more about my new friend.'

His words sent her heart into a wild dance while her face creased with worry.

'People aren't always what they seem.'

'Exactly, which is why I must know more about you.'

'Will I lose my job if you don't like what you find?' she asked boldly. 'Of course,' he replied swiftly.

His lips twitched and she knew that he was laughing at her.

CHAPTER TEN

The sale went ahead without trouble and the horsebox arrived from Martin's at ten o'clock that morning. Frances paced round and round her room rehearsing again and again what she would say to Kane.

They had dined together the evening before and he had kissed her good-night. Later this morning they were to drive up together to see the Truscotts.

Somehow she must tell him that she had bought Firefly and was now unable to go back to Tenerife. She would be needed here to get Firefly back into shape to race again. Martin had agreed to house him but the rest she must do for herself.

Lunchtime came and went and still there was no word from Kane, and there was no reply when she rang his room number. She rang reception to see if there was a message for her and was astounded when told that Mr Harding had settled up his bill and left.

There had to be some sort of mistake, surely. Even if something had come up that needed his attention he would hardly have left without leaving a message. Checking her room to make sure she had all her belongings, she picked up her bag and went down to reception.

Yes, her room had been paid for, and, yes, there was something waiting for her. She was handed a newspaper, and an envelope. Taking them across to a seat she sat down and opened the letter. It said simply that as she would see if she read the paper, his business deal with the German and French companies was off and he now had proof that she had sold him out to buy Firefly from Senora Mendoza.

He was saddened to remember that she had warned him that all was not as it seemed and she was right in her assumption that he would no longer require her assistance in Tenerife.

Stuffing the letter into her pocket, she pulled open the newspaper and on the business page, ringed in pen for her convenience, was the article he referred to. She read it repeatedly then slowly the paper crumpled to her knees. How could he believe she was capable of such treachery? He said he had proof. Why hadn't he stayed to face her with this so-called proof? She knew she had done nothing to be ashamed of. He had asked her to keep his deal a secret and she had told no-one. So where was his proof?

From horror, her emotions had turned to anger. Good riddance to him if that is what he thinks of me, she told herself, as a silent tear teetered on the edge of her lower lid. It made her life easier now she didn't have to tell him that she was staying in England. She ordered a taxi to the railway station and while she waited, she phoned Tessa to check that they had room for her. Thankfully she had never mentioned the possibility of Kane accompanying her to Yorkshire.

*   *   *

Two weeks passed and she rode Firefly out with the exercise string of horses every morning. His lameness had passed quickly and he was settling back nicely into racing routines. It was as if he knew he was back where he belonged, for he lost his timidity and wariness. His coat shone and his spirited demeanour returned as his head hung over the stable door calling and begging for titbits from passers-by.

It was just after the mid-day feed, halfway through the third week of Frances's return, that Martin called her into the office to take a telephone call. Lifting her brows in question she took the receiver from him.

'Hello.'

There was a lot of static then it cleared and Gilbert's voice came over the line.

'Fran, it is Gilbert. We have much trouble here.'

Again there was static and she could hardly hear him.

'I phone from a public box,' he said and she heard money going in. 'I cannot phone from the ranch. Kane has forbidden it. He has lost much money but here we all know it is not of your doing. This trouble comes from the Senora Mendoza and that Maurice. It is what we feared. It is why Juan Carlos also was forbidden to visit the ranch because the senora many years ago spoke that Juan Carlos was the son of Kane. He is not, but how you say it, mud sticks and Senor Kane is a proud man.'

The static was very bad for a few seconds and she missed what he said next. She strained her ears to catch his next words.

'Please, Fran, you will come,' was all she heard.

'I'm sorry, Gilbert, I didn't catch all that.'

He repeated what he had said and asked her again to come back to the ranch.

'I cannot come, Gilbert, I'm sorry. I swear to you I did nothing wrong but if Kane can hold Juan Carlos's birth against the boy for so long what hope have I of proving my innocence?'

When she had replaced the receiver, she stood with her hand resting on it for some time. So the only thing Juan Carlos had done was to have been the cause of some gossip years ago! With a sigh she turned to go to find Martin watching her from the doorway. He made a rueful face at her.

'Bad news?' he asked.

She shrugged.

'Someone from the Tenerife ranch wanting

me back.'

'Want to talk about it?'

She smiled.

'Some other time.'

He nodded and watched her leave the office and head for Firefly's box. Tessa had mentioned that Fran seemed troubled, though she was thoroughly enjoying being around the baby. One of the grooms called him from the top yard and all thoughts of Fran were forgotten.

*   *   *

'You just look after Firefly. There will be plenty of time later to think about racing.'

Martin was laying down the law to Fran who sent a pleading look to Tessa as she entered the kitchen.

'I must earn my keep somehow. If I thought for a moment I couldn't then I would never have come back.'

'Martin is right, Fran. It's far too soon to race again.'

'My arms have made good progress in the heat of Tenerife,' she objected.

She was angry and frustrated. She knew her friends were mystified at this impatient, different side to her character, but she couldn't help herself.

'What is it, Fran? What's really wrong?' Tessa asked in concern.

Martin had left the room and the two women sat side by side on the settle in front of the range.

'I don't know.' Frances sniffed. 'I just hated leaving Kane under such a cloud. How could he have believed what he did of me? I mean, I thought we were beginning to know each other.'

'I thought he was just unpleasant to you.'

'Yes, he was in the beginning,' Frances agreed.

'But things changed?'

Frances sighed.

'Yes.'

'And now what he thinks of you matters very much.'

Frances raised her head and stared at her friend. Knowledge flowed through her. I love him, she thought. I love him and he's in trouble. She rose from the seat and moved towards the table in the centre of the room where she turned back to her friend.

'I love him,' she said simply.

Tessa nodded. 'Of course you do.'

'I can't go back.'

'No, I don't suppose you can.'

'What do I do, Tessa? I've tried to put it behind me and look forward, but it's like a bad taste in my mouth which taints everything.'

'Well, you're not responsible, so who is? You must have some idea who could have seen those documents and informed the Press.'

Frances returned to her seat.

'Oh, I know who is behind it all right but even if I went back there, there is no saying I could prove anything.'

'You know, Fran, Firefly has made a better recovery from his sojourn in Tenerife than you have. Where's all the fight that made you such a successful jockey? You have changed so much I barely recognise you.'

Frances took up her friend's challenge, straightened her shoulders, gave one long sigh and smiled.

'Sorry to have been such a misery but I really will have to get back on track soon.'

'Of course you will, just not quite yet. And don't worry, Fran. Time will solve your problem for you, one way or another.'

The next morning, Frances held back from joining the string of horses going for exercise, waiting for their return before taking Firefly up on to the moors. The sun was burning off the last of the early mist and there was little wind. Only the piercing cry of the curlew broke the silence.

Her stillness communicated itself to the horse and together they rested. After a while, Firefly became restless and she nudged him forward on to the grassy track. He needed no encouragement. They were off, flying over the grass, the soft thud of his hooves music in her ears. All too soon it was over and she sat back in the saddle with a happy laugh. He was ready, she was sure of it. He was entered for a hurdle next month and by then she would be ready also.

The early-morning traffic was increasing as they made their way back through the village. A large white van was following them, unable to pass because of on-coming traffic. At the first sign of a gap, Frances waved him on, but he cut in very close leaving Frances no option but to climb on to the pavement, frightening the life out of a mother and baby who immediately crushed into a shop doorway, the pavement was so narrow.

Firefly danced on the spot until they moved back on to the road, then down into the stable yard. It wasn't until she had jumped down and was leading the horse into his box that she felt a twinge in her arm. She untacked him and was making her way across the yard to the tack room when, without warning, the saddle slid from her arm. Startled, she stood and stared at it for several minutes until someone shouted to her.

Martin was standing in front of her with the saddle in his hands, two of the lads down the yard watching. She smiled and, taking the saddle from Martin, walked on, but that night, she hardly slept for the pain in her arm. She remembered the van's mirror knocking her elbow as it passed but felt certain that if she rested it all would be well.

For the next few days, she said nothing to anyone about her injured arm but wore an elastic bandage on it to save it from unnecessary strain while she worked, but at night it continued to break her sleep.

As the day of her first race meeting since her accident nearly two years earlier drew nearer her arm continued to ache, no worse but no better. She carried on as usual in the yard and slept with the aid of painkillers at night.

There had been no more word from Tenerife and Frances had tried to smother her worry with work. She searched all the riding magazines for word of Kane, but never found anything. She read through all the financial pages she could find, trying to discover what was happening with the companies Kane had hoped to deal with, but there was nothing there either.

Now, the day of her big moment dawned and Firefly was as ready as he would ever be.

'Dancing out of his skin,' Tes sa grumbled as she and Frances watched him being boxed.

'If he's too much for her she'll let him go. She's promised me,' Martin said as he joined them.

Tessa gave Frances a stern look.

'Did you?'

She nodded.

'Well, make sure you do. The last thing we

want is you ending up back where we started two years ago.'

Martin gave his wife a kiss and climbed into the touring van that passed as Frances's changing-room on the course. Frances climbed in beside him and with a wave they were off. Martin had two horses that afternoon but one of the other jockeys was riding the second horse and had gone ahead in the box with the driver.

Halfway down the road, Martin's mobile went off.

'Here, you answer it,' he said pulling it from his pocket and tossing it to Frances.

'Hello? It's Tessa and she wants you.'

'Well, she can't have me. Doesn't she know its illegal now to use the phone on the road?'

'She says it's important. You'll have to pull over.'

'Drat the woman. Won't you do?'

'Apparently not.'

'We're in heavy traffic. Tell her she'll have to wait and I'll ring her back.' Frances passed on the message, then said, 'She said to be quick.'

'Fancy a bite to eat?' he asked as he pulled into a pub parking area a few miles down the road.

They left the van and made their way inside. It was early for lunch but the barmaid promised them a sandwich in five minutes. The race wasn't until two and it was only a half hour's drive farther on. Martin bought them both a drink then went off to return Tessa's call. When he came back, Frances thought he was unusually quiet and asked him if anything was wrong. He immediately cheered up.

'No, nothing important'

It had sounded pretty important to Tessa, she thought, but as the sandwiches arrived, the phone call was forgotten.

They arrived at the course not long afterwards and Martin buzzed around like a hungry bee, as Frances went to collect her gear. He shepherded her back to the van to change, hung around while she got ready and then walked down to the paddock with her. Frances assumed it was all on account of Tessa making him promise to look after her.

Normally she wouldn't have seen him until they met in the paddock prior to the race. Today she put up with his fussing for she felt in need of all the reassurance she could muster. She had taken two strong painkillers and wrapped her arm in elastic bandage. The rest was up to her knowledge of the horse she was riding and her skill at communicating with him.

The sun came out as they walked towards the paddock. The owners of Martin's second horse came out to meet him. They swarmed, questioned and dispersed as other trainers demanded his attention and Frances carried on alone to Firefly's side. He was tossing his head and sidling this way and that. People parted around him, keeping out of the way of his hind legs as Frances came up to him and took hold of the bridle. Now he stood still and dropped his head as she pulled his ears and whispered to him.

Soon it was time to mount up and the groom gave her a leg up while Martin double-checked girth and stirrup. She checked her chin strap and took up the reins. Her silks were purple with white bands and when she pulled her goggles down and adjusted them, she looked no different from any of the other jockeys preparing to go down to the start.

As she moved out on to the track and trotted down the rail, an ugly face with panhandle ears seemed to stare up at her for a moment then was gone as she passed.

I am seeing things now, she thought, and the shock released her body from tension and she relaxed into the saddle as Firefly cantered forward.

When the race started, they were out in front far too soon as Firefly flew over yet another hurdle. Tessa was right—he was too strong for her so she gave him his head and let him go.

Her injured arm lay virtually useless along his neck. However, there was nothing wrong with her legs and her voice as she called to him and encouraged him. With two more hurdles to go he was in the lead. Frances's heart raced with him. In seconds, another horse was alongside him. They jumped together, Firefly landing just inches ahead.

At the last, Firefly pecked and his head went down. Frances threw her body weight back along the saddle and with a grunt he was up and running again. Their rival was two lengths ahead of them and the thunder of following horses sounded terribly close when Frances called for that last bit of effort.

The ears in front of her twitched and she laughed in her throat as his stride lengthened and she thought he was going to bite the rump of the horse in front as they closed the gap. Then they were in the lead again . . .

'You won, you really won,' Martin shouted at her as they headed for the winners' enclosure.

Once there, she popped a leg over the horse's back and slid down to the ground. She pulled off the saddle and stepped back as a blanket was thrown over his back. For a moment, the press of the crowd and the excited noise of the congratulations all became a bit too much, leaving her feeling giddy and lightheaded. Then the pain kicked in and she nearly fainted.

Somehow she managed to smile and nod as she made her way to the weighing room. Then it was back to the van to change before she was headed back into the paddock for interview and photographs.

Wearily she pulled open the van door and climbed inside, closing the door just as someone inside the van stood up. With a groan her knees buckled and all went black . . .

When she opened her eyes it was to those same white walls and green curtains that had become so familiar to her in the weeks after her injury. But that was two years ago. What was she doing here now? A shadow passed across the window and she narrowed her eyes against the glare.

Kane was standing looking down at her, his expression serious, his eyes like dark green velvet showing only concern. Her bad arm was wrapped from shoulder to wrist as he took her good hand in his and said, 'Don't ever frighten me like that again.'

A smile quivered along her mouth.

'I would never have betrayed you.'

'I know that now and I am here to apologise. May I sit down? I would like to explain.'

She nodded her head, unable to believe that he was here. He pulled a chair up to the bed and sat down, taking her hand back into his. He began to talk softly, his eyes full of pain.

'When I was young, my mother left me in the care of a bitter, old man who didn't care about what I did or where I went. So I took

111

what I wanted from life and gave nothing in return. I learned from him to seek only self gratification and care about no-one. Then my mother returned and for the first time I looked for some sort of . . .'

He stumbled and Frances was sure it was because he couldn't bring himself to say the word love.

'I looked for attention, but she brought with her strangers who already had her devotion. Pilar was a young wife at this point, newly-married to an older man, but it didn't stop us having an affair. My newly-acquired stepsister was flirtatious and dangerously possessive. When she became pregnant, Pilar accused me. She was very jealous. When Isabella died later in mysterious circumstances, I came under suspicion and was sent away to Germany.

'I'm afraid I find personal relationships difficult and it was the easy way out to believe Pilar when she reminded me how often I had seen you with Beckwith. She also showed me a fax to the Press, supposedly from you. She told me how much Firefly had cost you and I couldn't come up with any other way you could have raised all that money on your own.'

Sighing heavily, Frances turned her hand beneath his and threaded her fingers through his.

'It took all my savings and some of Martin's as well.'

'After Gilbert's unsuccessful call to you, he

and Connie decided to put their heads together and came up with some questionable evidence that Pilar was behind the death of Isobella. The police are taking an interest at this moment. Pilar has gone to visit relatives in Brazil and I think she will take her time in coming back. Beckwith has vanished. So now I am able to ask you sincerely to forgive me.'

'You are forgiven,' Frances whispered with a smile.

'Now what is all this business about racing with a damaged arm?'

'We won,' she said in defiance, a grin spreading across her face. He was nodding.

'And you were wonderful. But you won't be racing again, at least not professionally. You will be too busy helping me to run the ranch in Tenerife.'

There was an awkward silence, broken only by the sounds of the hospital beyond the door. Frances chewed on her lower lip.

'I'm afraid . . .'

He leaned forward and kissed her gently.

'I want you to marry me.'

Her heart nearly stopped.

'Marry you? But Firefly . . .'

'I'm quite capable of taking care of Firefly,' Martin said, as he and Tessa came into the room, bringing a sheepish Gilbert with them.

'I tried to warn you but his lordship here decided it was better to make you wait,' Tessa said, 'and look what happened! You fainted

113

with shock.'

'She won,' Martin argued.

Tessa pushed him aside and draped herself over Frances, giving her a hug.

'So can I be matron of honour?'

Frances laughed and locked eyes with Kane.

I love you, their glances said.

'I'd love to have you as my matron of honour.'

When they had gone some time later, Kane remained and taking her in his arms held her close.

'About Juan Carlos,' she said, 'he has so much promise, Kane. Couldn't you see your way clear to allow him to come back to the ranch?'

'When you look at me like this I can deny you nothing but Gilbert has been before you and we shall see the boy's rise to success together.'

'Then my answer, which I haven't given yet, will be, when do we fly home?'

Chivers Large Print Direct

If you have enjoyed this Large Print book and would like to build up your own collection of Large Print books and have them delivered direct to your door, please contact **Chivers Large Print Direct**.

Chivers Large Print Direct offers you a full service:

✧ **Created to support your local library**

✧ **Delivery direct to your door**

✧ **Easy-to-read type and attractively bound**

✧ **The very best authors**

✧ **Special low prices**

For further details either call Customer Services on 01225 443400 or write to us at

Chivers Large Print Direct
FREEPOST (BA 1686/1)
Bath
BA1 3QZ